One Good Thing About America

RUTH FREEMAN

Holiday House • New York

Acknowledgments

This story has been helped and inspired by many people. I am deeply grateful, first of all, to the students I have worked with at Skillin Elementary School in South Portland, Maine, and King Middle School in Portland. Thank you to the wonderful teachers (especially the ELL department) and staff in the South Portland School District and to Marcia Salem, English Language Learning teacher extraordinaire, who took me on as an intern.

I spoke to two people in Portland who are dedicated to helping newcomers: Jeff Tardiff, director of Portland's Family Shelter, and Sue Roche, director of the Immigrant Legal Advocacy Project (ILAP). Both were generous with their time and experience while patiently answering my questions.

I was sure this story was going to be a picture book. It was Mary Cash, my editor at Holiday House, who kept asking for more pages. First she wanted 50 more pages. When I handed them in, she wanted 30 more. And, when they were done, she asked for a few more to answer the last lingering questions. She has pushed and pulled this story into the shape it is now. It simply wouldn't be what it is without her.

The publisher thanks Professor William Foster III for his expert sensitivity review.

Copyright © 2017 by Ruth Freeman
All Rights Reserved
HOLIDAY HOUSE is registered in the U.S. Patent and Trademark Office.
Printed and bound in February 2017 at Maple Press, York, PA, USA.
www.holidayhouse.com
First Edition
1 3 5 7 9 10 8 6 4 2

Library of Congress Cataloging-in-Publication Data
Names: Freeman, Ruth, 1951- author.
Title: One good thing about America / by Ruth Freeman.
Description: First edition. | New York : Holiday House, [2017] | Summary:
"Anais, who has recently emigrated from Africa to Maine with her mother
and young brother, copes with acclimating herself to a new country,
understanding American culture, learning English, figuring out how to fit
in at school, and moving from motel to shelter and finally to a permanent
apartment"—Provided by publisher.
Identifiers: LCCN 2016027037 | ISBN 9780823436958 (hardcover)
Subjects: | CYAC: Immigrants—Fiction. | Africans—United States—Fiction. |
Family life—Fiction. | Homeless persons—Fiction. | English language—Fiction.
Classification: LCC PZ7.1.F7547 On 2017 | DDC [Fic]—dc23 LC record available
at https://lccn.loc.gov/2016027037

To my students

• ○ ☆ • ☆ ○ •

September 14

Dear Oma,

We go to my new school today. It is VERY BIG. Mama
and me and Jean-Claude we walk from the motel and
find school. Mama write and write many papers for the
school. A man come. He speak English and French and
help us. I tell Jean-Claude to stay calm but he is bad boy.
A lady bring the crayons and I tell Jean-Claude to play
with them.

Many many children are in the school. 400 say the
man. Yes 400. Vraiment. Really. It is like the city. And
my school at home in Congo is like one little house.
I tell the man I get lost. He say I do not. I get lost. I
know it.

We sit at table in little room a long long time. The
students go by and look at me. Also they mayke noise.
A big noise all the time. I do not like my new cloze. The

man say the word is itch. He write it for me. My new clothes itch. I am nine years old so I am in the forth grade say the man. I hope that is good. I tell Mama to tell the man I am good student but she does not no the English. I no many more English than Mama. I tell the man I am good student. I go tomorrow for my first day of school. This night I am talking in mirror in bathroom and saying Hello Good morning Hello Please Thank you. Jean-Claude think I am funny. I teach him to say Hello My Name is Jean-Claude. He think he is funny now also.

We miss are friends. We stay in a room in there apartment when they get us at Boston airport but they need the room so now the shelter people put us in motel. We have two big beds and a bathroom. Soon we will move to apartment in shelter. Move move move.

I miss my old house. I miss the mango tree with my tree house. I miss you and my friends. I miss Papa and Olivier. Do you hear from Papa? Mama and I worry for him very much. I look out the window to see the stars. Les étoiles is much more pretty word than stars I think. You tell me before I leave home les mêmes étoiles the same stars look down on you and me and they take care of me like you take care of me. I want the stars to take care of you and Papa and Olivier. But I no see stars.

Why do you say I have to write in English? You can not read it but have to take my letter to my old teacher to read for you. Please let me use le français. I am very tired with English today.

Mama tell me to write hello. Hello.
Bisous,

Anaïs

September 15

Dear Oma,

Ok I go to my new school this day. Mama and Jean-Claude take me. I do not want to go. I stand outside and Mama talk to me. Talk talk talk. I not go in. A lady come. She open the door. Mama give me hug and push. I am not happy. Not not not happy.

In the BIG school I get lost. I know it. No one speak our langage. I meet my new teacher. Miss smile and say many words. Very fast. A long long river of words. Mabe English mabe not. I not know what Miss say. I say yes yes yes. One student think my name is Yes. I tell the class my name one two three times. The students say my name but it not sound like my name. No one can say

Anaïs. Miss say How Do You Spell That? Miss ask if she can call me Annie. I want to say no but the words do not come fast from my mouth. I am Annie now.

I am happy to go home and stop the yes yes yes. I am happy to be Anaïs again. It is good to be with Mama in the room at motel. I even am glad to see Jean-Claude. I am nice to him and play with him. Our friends bring us food and we eat with them. I do not eat the food in school. Do you no Americans eat fingers from chickens and sticks from fish? Now I no Americans are very very CRAZY. Complètement fou!

Do you hear about Papa? I hope he is safe. Mama say I can not write very much about him because it is not safe to put things in letters about him. In case a bad man see my letter. I hope Papa and Olivier come to America soon. If they come to America then you are all alone. I think mabe you need me to come live with you. Please tell Mama I can come. You are my Mama's Mama and she listen to you. I take care of you and cook for you and we talk together. I tell you stories of CRAZY AMERICA.

Bisous,

Anaïs

Dear Oma,

Ok school is no good. You no when I get first in
English at my school at home? Tell my teacher
Monsieur I speak English here but the teachers and the
students look at me like I am crazy. Me? But I want to
say I am not the crazy one. I feel like the baby of my
auntie. So I say no thing. I look and look at the faces.
I am like a big cat with yellow eyes. I try to read what
the faces say but the words go to fast. The words go like
the wind and I can not catch them.

I can do nothing so I go to the machine with a hole.
It take pencils and make them good. It is fun and make
BIG NOISE. My teacher tell me to sit down. But I have
to raise my hand and ask for the batroom. Miss do not
know what I say. I say I have to pee. The students think
it funny. Now I do not like English no no way.

It is much much better if I live with you. Here in
the motel it is no home. I do not have my friends or
the little yellow and black birds in my mango tree. If
I live with you I sweep and work in your garden and
make you tea. Olivier is with you but he is 15 now and

is no good for cooking and making tea. I can tell you stories of crazy America and make you laugh. Do you miss me? Please let me come.

Bisous,

Anaïs

September 20

Dear Oma,

I am very happy to get letter from you! And thank you to Monsieur for writing it! I am happy you are well. But you and Mama say I have to work hard and write you in English? And now you and Monsieur say I have to find one good thing about America every day? This is a very hard job. Or maybe impossible! It is much better to find good things about home with you like your bananes plantain that I miss very very much.

There are many many hard things about America because English is a CRAZY language. The letters we call voyelles are vowels here. They are a e i o u. They always are sounding different! And I am sorry to say they are in every word. Miss say they are tricky. They always are changing like snakes. The tricky vowels are in the students names like Jayden Jaylene Januel Josiah Joshua Jordan Jenna Jayla Jacob. I think Americans like names to start with J.

Please write to Mama and tell her you want me to go home. Then I do not have to learn all these J names.

Ok I want to go home with you but I tell you one good thing for today. In America students wear no uniform. I wear my new clothes that itch. The students ware diffrent clothes and backpacks. My teacher give me a backpack today. She look happy when she give me the pink backpack. It had a girls name in it. I give it back to her. I hate pink. She look sad but then she give me a black backpack. It has a yellow and black bird on it. I remember the yellow and black birds at home when I see it. Jenna say the bird is called a batman bird. I love my new backpack!!!!

If you talk to Papa please tell him we are good. Tell him we miss him! Olivier too. Is Olivier liking his school? Tell Olivier to write me a letter. In English! Do not tell him but sometime it is a little bit nice to not have a big brother to tell me what to do. I am the oldest one now!

Bisous,

Anaïs

September 22

Dear Oma,

Today was a bad day. We have to hurry to line up for
PE the same word for the gym and the same word for
the cafeterya. Jenna say I cut her. I did not. I promise.
My teacher tell me to go to the end of the line. I do not
know why Jenna say I cut her. I had no thing to cut her
with!

Jenna look mad at PE and recess. I look mad at her.
At lunch she spill her milk and I laff. It is funny. So she
hit me and I hit her. Jenna is not a nice girl. In the
classroom Miss make us sit at Quiet Island. It is a
table where bad students go.

I am sorry but I cannot think of one good thing
about America today. But I will be a good girl if I live
with you. I will be so so good. I will be good better
best! If I live with you I never have to go to Quiet Island
again.

Bisous,

Anaïs

September 25

Dear Oma,

Miss tell me today I have the best handwriting in the class! This is one good thing for sure! I write the way Monsieur was teaching us. In America they call it kursiv. The students think it is hard. I say it is the way we write all the time in my old school. They tell me to write more but I dont know what to say so I write in French. But they can not read it so they dont like it I think. Jenna is still looking mad at me.

There is a table by the school door with clothes on it. It is the Lost and Found place. There are so many lost clothes! I tell Miss I can find them! I can maybe find jackets for me and Jean-Claude but Miss say no. She say the clothes are waiting for other students to find them. I don't understand. I tell Mama and Jean-Claude about the Lost and Found. Jean-Claude stops his playing and asks Mama if we are lost. She look at me and then smiles at him and we play a game. She tells me to hide in the motel room and she and Jean-Claude find me. Then Jean-Claude hides. It is funny. Every time he hides under the bed. It is our new Lost and Found game.

Mama go to her first English class today. It is a school for mothers and fathers and aunties and uncles. She put Jean-Claude in one room to play with the children and she go to another room. She say it is hard. She miss her work selling fruits and vegetables at the market in the city. She miss seeing all her friends. But here there is no work until Mama learn English and get the papers. Maybe nobody tells you and Mama before that America is a hard place to live. The only easy thing for me is writing kursiv.

Bisous,

Anaïs

September 28

Dear Oma,

Thank you so many many times for the phone call! It is so so good to talk to you! Do not worry about Jenna. She is my best friend now. She is a nice girl. We play the game with string in our hands like I play at home! Jenna lets me cut in front when we line up. She is my good friend and the one good thing about America for today. But not Januel. I am happy to say I raise my hand today and say one answer. But Januel ask why I talk funny. This is not good funny but bad funny. Miss talk to him but no matter. My English is no good. I will be a Quiet Island now even when I don't go there.

We are moving soon. We will go to the shelter to a room for us now. It will be good for Mama to have a place to cook. Mama tried to call Papa to tell him we are moving but Papas phone did not work. She will try to call him again but if you can please tell him where we are. Tell him I go to a big school and I work hard. Tell him and Olivier I will take the bus to school.

I like to write to you even if you make me write in English. I see you taking my letter down the road to my old school where Monsieur will read my words to you. Do you see my old house? Is my tree house still in the mango tree? I want to sit in it and listen to the yellow and black birds. No person say they talk funny.

Mama say we have been in America for one month now.

Bisous,

Anais

October 1

Dear Oma,

Here is one little letter before I go to bed. It is about one more crazy thing they do here in America! Every day in school we pray like in my school at home. But we pray to the flag. Over the loud box come voices of students and we say with them words about the God that is invisible. That is one word I know now. Invisible. Miss say it mean something we don't see. Sometimes I think I will like to be invisible very much. They do not say Amen. They say Please Be Seated Thank You And Have a Nice Day. Many people in America say Have A Nice Day all the time. Maybe it is the crazy America way for Amen. I do not know.

The way Jean-Claude say my name it sound like Nice! Tonite he say Nice Nice he say he want to play the Lost and Found game. I tell him he is learning English because he know the word for Nice! He don't understand what I am telling him.

Bisous et Bonne Nuit!

Anaïs

Dear Oma,

Papa calld!!! We are so so happy to hear his voice. He did not tell us where he is. He talk to Mama for a long time. Mama say to me when Jean-Claude is asleep that it is hard for Papa because the soldiers are looking for him because the mining company say he is a bad man and took something from them but we know he is a good man. The good better best manager! But they don't believe him and he is scared they put him in jail or hurt him. Mama say there are crazy things going on in our country. I ask again please please please if I can go live with you. Mama said no. Again. She say she will be so sad if I was in some other place and it is not safe. She say it is not safe for us to stay there. That is why we have to leave. Mama say America is our home now.

Mama say you and she want me to learn English and go to school and do things that she was not ever doing. She say she was sorry not to have many years in school like me. She even say it is maybe good to make my name Annie like an American girl. I do not think I can be an American girl. Annie in Crazy America is not me. Anaïs in Africa. That is me. I miss the smell of your cooking fire. I miss the stars smiling and taking care of you and me. I miss your garden and my tree house in the mango tree and my home and my friends so so much. Here Mama does not let me to go outside by myself.

We live now at the shelter. We have a kitchen with the family Omar and the family Potter. The family Omar do not like the family Potter and the family Potter do not like the family Omar. There is a lot of cooking. We learnd about the smoke detector box in the top of the kitchen. It makes a VERY LOUD bell sound. Now Jean-Claude is afraid to go to the kitchen.

Today I take the bus 23 to school at 8:05 for the first time. Mama and me and Jean-Claude wait on the street in the morning with the Omar family. There are two little Omar girls at my school. Noor is in 2 grade and Riham is in kindrgarten. They speak Arabic and a little bit English. I think Jean-Claude will like to play with Riham because she is only two years older than him. We are very early because Mrs. Omar say to Mama Giselle we can not be late because the bus will not wait. She showd Mama the 8:05 on her clock. Americans are crazy about clocks and being ON TIME.

Today I go see a new teacher Ms. Taylor for English. It was a different part of the school and I am lost. Again. A nice man was cleaning the floor. There was some crying in my eyes I think. He help me find Ms. Taylor. He speaks French! He is calld Mr. Dan. He was a teacher of languages in his country. I was so happy to talk French with him! Mr. Dan is the good better best thing about America today!

Bisous,

Anaïs

October 6

Dear Oma,

Ms. Taylor is my new teacher for English. I leave my class and go to see her every day. She help me learn English and I help her to learn to say Anaïs. She cannot speak French but she is very pretty. She is brown like we are. She say she is from an island called Road Island. Do you know it? Is it in Africa? Mama do not know it. Ms. Taylor say Cool! when she like something and Bingo! when I get right answer.

When I tell Mama and Jean-Claude about Ms.

Taylor at dinner Jean-Claude say brown people speak French and white people speak English. Jean-Claude has to learn very much before he can go to school.

Today Ms. Taylor give me a test to see how many English words I have. I tell her I was best student in English at my old school. The test was hard. I have to say words to a computer and write and listen. I want to do so so well. She say Good Job many times but I don't know if it was really good job. Americans in school say Good Job a lot!

Ms. Taylor say English is a crazy language. I tell her I think so too! She is trying to learn more Spanish so she know another language is hard. She make me feel better.

She get a map and we find Congo and we find Maine. She ask about my family so I tell her. She ask if I can draw a picture. I draw my house and your house close to ours on the big road on its way into the city. And your garden and the tree where you sit and drink tea. And my tree house in the mango tree. I tell her about Papa and when he was fighting with the army and hurt his leg but then the government got him a good job working for the mining company. I tell her he was triying to help the boys and men who work so hard but the company didn't like what he did and call him a bad man and now they want to put him in jail. I tell her we don't know where he is now. I tell her about Mama and her selling fruits and vegetables in the market in the city. And about Olivier wanting to leave school to help Papa but you and Mama wanting him to stay with you so he can stay in school.

I talk so much to Ms. Taylor! I wish you can see her. I'm saying she is one good thing about America today for sure!

Bisous,

Anaïs

October 10

Dear Oma,

Ms. Taylor help me write my letter today to the Student of the Week. We do this every week in my regular class. Some week it is going to be my turn to get letters! Today I write to Brittany. I do not know her very good at all. Here is my letter:

Dear Brittany,

You are a nice girl. You help me with the morning message when I don't know what it say to do. You are good in sports too. I like your hair. I wish I had your hair.

Your friend, Annie

Brittany has long yellow hair like on the TV. Ms. Taylor say she think my hair is beautiful too. I say Mama did my braids. She say my hair is VERY COOL! She has short hair. I tell her she needs braids. She say maybe she will get them. She say braids look so cool because there are so many styles. She show me how to spell styles.
I draw her pictures of the styles I know and she draw pictures of the styles she know. We use lots and lots of paper. Next time I think I will ask Mama to give me hair xtenshuns. Right now I have braids that hang down to my ears with little beads on each one. I love the noise they make when I move.

Ms. Taylor and I say hair is one good thing about America today! But then I think we have hair at home in Congo too.

Bisous,

Anaïs

October 15

Dear Oma,

I am learning about Halloween in America. Miss talks about it and I say yes yes but I don't know what she say. The stories we read now are about scary things. Today we have to write about something scary. I was thinking for a long time. I was thinking what can I write. I was thinking of the soldiers with guns outside my house when they come looking for Papa. And when they get mad at Mama asking her where he is. And then they look every place in our house even my tree house in the mango tree. They turn things over and break our things. Olivier is a brave boy but the soldiers push him away with their guns. They tell us they will come back.

Jenna was writing about a scary pumpkin monster outside her house. She was drawing rainbows and hearts and flowers on her house. So I write about a scary pumpkin monster outside my house and put rainbows and hearts and flowers like Jenna.

When Jean-Claude wake up with a bad dream Mama tell him we are safe now. No bad people will come here. She tell me too. I know we are safe at the shelter but it is no home like our old home. And when

Mr. Potter is yelling or the little Omar girls are crying it does not feel good here. I don't tell Mama but I am afraid we never have a home again like our old home.

Ok I am trying to think of one good thing for today. I do not like the Halloween but I will tell you I love the leaves. They come down from trees like rain. The air smells like the honey in your house and the leaves when you walk on them make the sound of eating toast. I want you to see all of this. You will love it.

The leaves
WHEN YOU WALK ON THEM MAKE THE SOUND OF EATING TOAST. YOU'LL LOVE IT!

I miss you so much and I hope you and Papa and Olivier are safe.

Bisous,

Anaïs

October 19

Dear Oma,

Thank you so much for your nice letter! And thank
Monsieur for writing it. If Miss see it she will say to
Monsieur best kursiv ever! Mama and me read your
words and you say we will find a home. It will be
different from our old home but you say the rite home is
waiting for us. And you say I will know it is the rite one
when I see it. I hope so.

Mama looks for an apartment. The people at the
shelter help her and also a woman Ms. Defazio about
getting a silum so we can stay in America. Ms. Defazio
helps Mama writing lots and lots of papers. I hope we
move. And I can take a big school bus and not the speshul
little one that goes only to the shelter. I will not be missing
the Potter family for sure. Every time we see Mr. Potter he
say Whadzup? The first time I lookd up to see and he was
thinking it was the most funny thing ever! Now he say
Whadzup every time he sees me and laffs very much.

In school today Januel was talking about something
he do after school. He was talking about it to Jenna and
me. Januel is not my friend but he is not still saying I
talk funny. He talked about this thing called the Poison

Girls Club. Jenna was thinking it was fun. Is she crazy I say? The Poison Girls Club? She lafft but it's ok when Jenna laffs now. It is really called the Boys and Girls Club. I am glad Januel didn't hear. I wish Americans are speaking English better!

POISON *girls* CLUB

There was chicken at lunch today but it looked like something from my nose. Really!! The rice was good but not as good as your rice. I miss the chicken you cook too and the frites.

Please write another letter and tell me what you are doing. I miss you.

Bisous,

Anais

October 22

Dear Oma,

I have a funny story to tell. The good kind of funny
and not the bad kind of funny. We have to write a story
today about the house we live in. Miss say to use words
to make a picture in our heads. She say I can write
about my house in Africa. So I think about our house
and tell her it was white. I have many more words to
say about my house but first she said I have to say as
white as something else. What something else is white
I am thinking? I remember the ground orange hot in
the sun and cool brown where the sun can not find it.
I remember the green leaves of the mango tree and the
mangos inside all yellow sweet. I remember the blue and
black of your best dress and the red and green of Mamas.
My teacher waited. As white as what she say. I look at
her and say as white as American people. Her eyes got
big bigger biggest! Then she lafft. The other students
wanted to hear. Miss ask if I can tell them what I say. I
did not know what to do. But I say my house is as white
as American people. Miss was laughing and the students
are laughing too. Jenna gave me a thumbs up. At lunch
Januel say I tell a good joke today in school. But he say

not all Americans are white. He talk talk talk but I don't understand his words. No matter. It was a good day. A great day. And funny too!

Most of the leaves are on the ground now. There are so many colors. Red brown yellow orange green. Even when it is cloudy it is like there is sunshine all over the ground. I want you to come visit us. We will show you where we live and feed you good food. I will ask Mama. Please come.

Bisous,

Anaïs

October 26

Dear Oma,

Papa call. We do not know where he is but he was hearing the soldiers went back to your house to look for him. Are you ok? And Olivier too? Mama and I are worrying a lot. I hope they did not hurt you or things in your house or your garden. We try to call you tonight but no anser. We hope we talk to you soon.

I wish you were here with us. You will see everything

in school now is orange and black for Halloween. And there are pumpkins and ghosts. Americans put scary faces on pumpkins. They don't eat the pumpkins and leaves like we do. They only make round pies and eat the seeds. Crazy Americans!

I tell Ms. Taylor about you. She likes hearing about you. I draw pictures of you working in your garden for her. We look at the map to see where you are.

To make you smile I will tell you I am making an idea about Ms. Taylor. Jenna and me are working for it. If you see me now you will see a big secret smile on my face. Ha ha! That is how Americans laff on paper!

We have math today. I love math because the numbers are the same as in my old school. Not like tricky words! Tell Monsieur when he reads this to you to remember how much I liked math! When I see you I will show you what I can do with numbers. I can write the biggest numbers like one hundred thousand million! And I am learning multiplication. Miss showd me that word today. Numbers are so fun! They are the good thing for today! But not story problems. The numbers hide inside lots of words about stickers or baseball. Story problems are stupid and not fun.

We do not get the apartment. Mama is looking for another one.

We say our prayers for Papa and you and Olivier tonight.

Bisous,

Anais

October 28

Dear Oma,

Mama tell me when I get home from school that she talkd to you today. She say to me that the soldiers did come to your house like Papa was hearing but I am so so glad to hear you are ok. But then she say they hurt Olivier. He was mad and trying to fite them and they got mad and are hitting and kicking him. Mama say he has many hurts on him and his arm is bad. She say you and Monsieur get a doctor to come take care of him. She say it is good they did not take him away but left him with you.

Please take good care of him. Tell him we are so sorry he is hurt and we cannot help him. Mama was talking to her friends on the phone tonight so I am putting Jean-Claude to bed. We are missing Olivier and Papa a lot. I tell him all the things I remember about Olivier. That he is tall and likes to be funny. He plays soccer with his friends but helps Jean-Claude learn to kick the ball too. I tell Jean-Claude that someday Olivier wants to build a big big hotel in Kisangani so that all the world will come and see our butiful country.

Then Jean-Claude wants to hear about Papa. So I tell him Papa is a good strong Papa who was a soldier and hurt his leg and then workd for the mine company. That is why he is not at home a lot. Mama comes to say goodnight. We talk about Papa. She is telling Jean-Claude about the mine where Papa workd. Mama gets her phone. See this she say? Inside here is a little bit of black rock. She calls it a mineral. She say her English teacher say it is the same word in French and English. It is what Papa workd so hard for at the mine. She lets Jean-Claude hold her phone. Then she shows him a picture of Papa in her phone.

We are missing each one of you tonight so so much.

Bisous,

Anaïs

November 1

Dear Oma,

Thank you for telling us Olivier is doing good. We are very happy to hear it! Tell him hello from us and maybe read my letter to him. It is all about Halloween!!! He will never be thinking what happen on Halloween last night so I will tell you. Mr. and Mrs. Potter say we have to go trik or treeting with them. They tell us it is good. It is fun. It is not bad. It is an American time when children put on clothes they call kostooms and get lots of candy! Yes lots and lots of candy! Mama and Mr. and Mrs. Omar talk and say ok. Mrs. Potter finds sheets to put on me and Jean-Claude and Noor and Riham so we look like ghosts. We wear our warm clothes under the sheets. Not too much sheet was left for Jean-Claude so he was a ghost in a little white jacket!

Mr. and Mrs. Potter have 2 big boys but they are going out with there friends. The big boys don't talk to us very much. Mr. and Mrs. Potter are nice to us and like jokes like Mr. Potter and Whadzup! I am thinking because it is Halloween and Mr. Potter likes candy that is why he wants us to go with him. Ha ha! Mr. Potter went outside with all us behind him. It was very dark and a little wet. It was a little scary to be out in the night. Mama was holding my hand and Jean-Claudes hand. And we have big shopping bags for candy. Mr. Potter stopped at each house with a pumpkin and was telling us to say Trik or Treet loud. We got candy from every one! I wish Olivier was here. He will love it. It was like a good dream! A best dream ever! So many kinds of candy. Jean-Claude did not say anything. He was really not believing it! I will ask Mama if we can send some candy to Olivier.

Then Mr. Potter said we can go to a better place with bigger houses for more candy. I am thinking we are going to have to give Mr. Potter a lot of our candy! Mama and Mr. and Mrs. Omar did not know about it but said ok. We walk a long way and Mama was carrying Jean-Claude. Mr. Omar was carrying Riham and Mrs. Omar and I hold Noors hands. The houses was getting bigger and there was trees. We find lots of pumpkin houses to go to. And there are other people dressing up and going trik or treeting too. It was so fun! With our sheets we lookd like all the other American ghosts and monsters. No one could see who we are! We got really good at saying Trik or Treet too like American kids.

We can see inside many houses because the lights

are on inside. One house had a big tree outside and a pumpkin in the window. And inside we can see stars! So many many stars. I can not believe it! I show Mr. Potter the stars in the room and he lafft at me. Again. He said they are tine lights. A nice woman opened the door with a big bole of candy. The room behind her was filled with the tine lights like stars. And there was many people in kostooms. Big people and children too. It looked so happy and warm. And there was a sofa and many books on shelves and pictures on the walls! Oma, I wanted to stay in that very beautiful room. I am thinking can we maybe find a room with stars someday to be warm and happy in? The candy was good but the room with stars was the better and best thing for today for sure!!!

christmas lights
I THINK THEY LOOK LIKE LITTLE STARS
(NOT REAL STARS BUT ALMOST)

We have a long walk home but I am thinking of the Halloween house with stars. It was a cloudy night and I do not see any stars. I miss the stars at home always looking down on me and on you. I will dream of a house with stars someday.

Bisous,

Anais

November 3

Dear Oma,

So much Halloween candy is in the freezer! Mama lets us have some candy every day. I think Mr. Potter is maybe eating a lot of it too. Every time I eat some candy I think of the warm Halloween house with stars.

There is a new girl in my class. Her name is Ikran. She is from Somalia. She is covered in a hijab. When she draws a picture of her family her Mama and little sisters look like bears. All covered up with two eyes. Januel askt why she wears it and why I don't wear it and if I know her in Africa. Really Januel I said? You think Africa is one small place? Januel is all the time putting his foot in it. This means the words come out before the thinking.

Ikran comes with me to Ms. Taylor's class. I show her where we go. We see Mr. Dan in the hallway. He is so nice. He says Bonjour Mademoiselle to me and to Ikran but she don't understand. She only knows Somali. Mr. Dan don't know Somali. He say he forgot to learn Somali. Also English. Now we are all having to learn English. We learn English in the day time at school. Mr. Dan learn English at night. I'm glad I don't go to school at night!

Ikran thinks Ms. Taylor can understand so she talks Somali. A lot of Somali. Ms. Taylor looks at me. We do not know what she is saying. At recess Ikran follows me and Jenna. If we run away she stands by herself and looks sad. Then we have to go back and play with her. Ikran will not eat lunch. She says it is haram which I know means not good. I tell her I did not eat lunch when I was new. I tell her I know it looks dégoutant. Disgusting. But it is ok. Really. It is good. Well it is good sometimes.

One good thing is that Jenna and I can talk about our secret for Ms. Taylor and Ikran don't know what we say. Ha ha. Ikran is a little bit annoying. This is a word Ms. Taylor told us today. It means énervant. Ok, Oma, I

can hear you telling me I have to be nice to Ikran.
I will try.

Bisous,

Anaïs

November 7

Dear Oma,
Mama is sitting at the table looking at the papers she
was writing with Ms. Defazio today. She say she must
do papers for a new apartment and papers to stay in
America. Ms. Defazio tell Mama she need papers saying
why we can't go back home. Papers saying the soldiers
and the mining company get mad at us and maybe
even hurt us. Mama tells her the soldiers go back to
your house again. It is not safe there. Olivier is hurt.
Mama will call you and try to talk to Papa somehow.
And Mama has homework papers for her English class.
There are papers for everything. Mama say we will get
an apartment soon. Then we will get papers so we can

stay here. Then she will get a paper so she can get a job. I am sitting here doing my math homework. More papers.

Jean-Claude is asleep in his bed. Mama and I sit at the table and have tea while we do our paper work. It is a nice time. It is not a real home but I am used to our room at the shelter now. And it is quiet now that the Potters and Omars are in their rooms.

Today in school a funny thing happened. Mrs. F came. She is a teacher who teaches us how to make friends and be nice. Today she had a story about fish. Fish you say? Yes she read us a story about a fish with many other fish. It was a school of fish! Ha ha! But this fish wanted her own PERSONAL SPACE. I know these words because we had to write them on the paper. Mrs. F had a picture of two bowls and many little orange fish. She askt us where will the little orange fish be happy? By itself or with many others? I was thinking it would be nice if they were all together. Just like Mama and Jean-Claude and me all together in our little room at the shelter. And it will be so good to have you Papa and Olivier here too! But this was the wrong answer! I learned today that Americans want PERSONAL SPACE. So the right answer was to put them far away from each other. I think Ikran looked a little sad too. If Ikran was a little orange fish I think she will want her little sisters and brothers very close with her. I know I will want you in my fish bowl with me. These crazy Americans!

Bisous,

Anaïs

November 10

Dear Oma,

Well I am sorry to say but today was a boring day in school. The word boring means ennuyeux. I learnd it today from Jenna. She said it is a boring day because everything was the same. Nothing happens. I was thinking about boring. And I was thinking is boring bad or good? I was thinking maybe sometimes boring is good. I like it when Monday is everytime PE. And Good goes with Morning. Recess goes with lunch. Bus 23 goes with 8:05. For Mr. Potter Whatz goes with Up. The same way in crazy English Q goes with U and T goes with H. Well not all the times. Every time I learn one rule it changes and there's a new rule.

The one good thing today was you and Olivier called us on Monsieur's phone! I am sorry when he was telling us his arm hurt but the doctors say it will be ok. Mama will take the pictures he was sending us of his arm to Ms. Defazio.

Tonight I playd with Noor and Riham. Mrs. Omar askt me to take them to our room and play with them while she and Mr. Omar went to the store. It was fun. We watched a video and I draw pictures for them. I read a book to them and Jean-Claude too. Mrs. Omar came back and gave me a big bag of chips. For just me! I eat some and will take some to school tomorrow for me and Jenna and Ikran. And Januel if he's nice. I love chips!

I *love* CHIPS!

Bisous,

Anaïs.

November 13

Dear Oma,

Today we are learning about the Pilgrims. I am so
happy to learn about the Pilgrims because they came
to America like us! They came on a little boat not a
plane like Mama and Jean-Claude and me. And they
did not come from Africa. I know they did not come
from Africa because they had so many clothes! I think
the Pilgrims turned into Americans so maybe I can too.
There was Native Americans too. They didn't wear many
clothes. And they are a little brown like us. Maybe I can
be a Native American but with more American clothes.

We learned Native Americans put a fish in a hole
to make their corn grow. I don't know why. They will
do better to watch you. You can grow anything in your
garden and you don't need a fish! If I meet a Native
American or a Pilgrim I will tell them to ask you about
your garden.

Ms. Taylor askt me and Ikran about our trips to
America because we are kind of like the Pilgrims she
said. She knows from Ikran's papers she came from a
refugee camp in Kenya. Ms. Taylor said to Ikran Kenya?
Refugee camp? And Ikran said yes yes and talked a lot.

In Somali. I tell about my trip with Mama and Jean-Claude. We take the plane from Kisangani to Kinshasa, the plane from Kinshasa to Paris, the plane from Paris to Boston and our friends car to Portland. 1, 2, 3 planes. I show them how Jean-Claude got sick on plane 1 and 2. And our friends car. Ms. Taylor said it is called throwing up. On plane 3 he was sleeping. I watched a movie. Then I wanted something to drink so they gave me a can. The lady open it and put it in a cup. I had some and was thinking I was going to DIE! It was the first time I had soda and it burned my inside! That was the first time I started to know Americans are crazy.

And I remember when the plane was coming to Boston. Mama said to me look look. The oshun! I have not seen the oshun and we are so so close to it I am thinking we will hit it! I think I am going to DIE again!

Ms. Taylor wants Ikran and me to write about our countries in Africa so we can tell our class. I colored a picture of our flag today. I ask Ms. Taylor about the Road Island that was her home. She said it was not in Africa and not an island! She was born in America! She is a real American! Ms. Taylor says I can be a real American too and I can learn English. Bingo! Ok but sometimes when teachers say things like that I don't know if maybe it is true or not. I still feel like an African girl.

Bisous,

Anaïs

November 16

Dear Oma,

I work on my report on our country. I will read it and show it to my class in a few days. Ms. Taylor helps me and Ikran. I know more English than Ikran so Ms. Taylor helps her a lot. I am getting to see pictures of our country on the computer. I love the computer. I know how to drag and drop and X out. The pictures of my country make me happy and sad. I look for you in the pictures but I do not see you yet.

Well here is the secret about Ms. Taylor. I was telling Jenna about Ms. Taylor one day. Jenna wants to come with me to Ms. Taylor's class because it is fun but she can not because she speaks English like a real American girl. But Jenna say Ms. Taylor is very cool! I think so too. Well because I meet Mr. Dan in the hall I can see Mr. Dan is a very nice man. And Ms. Taylor is a very nice woman. And pretty. So I think they can meet and like each other. Jenna likes this idea. She says we have a PLAN.

At recess we work on our PLAN. Ikran comes too but can't understand what we say. We hold up two fingers. We say Mr. Dan! Ms. Taylor! Friends? We are thinking of how to do our plan. Jenna say maybe Mr. Dan can be like a superhero and save Ms. Taylor from some bad guys. But then I say where and how for goodness sake do we get bad guys? Miss always is saying for goodness sake! We need a new PLAN.

Then we play on the monkey bars. I am getting really good like a real monkey! Ha ha! But then I fall and hurt my knee. Ikran goes with me to the nurse. She follows me all the afternoon and points to my knee and speaks Somali like a little mama. I think she must take care of her little brothers and sisters at home a lot. It is good she has to go home to her little brothers and sisters or I think she would come home to take care of me!

How are you? How is your garden? Do you know anything about Papa? But I remember Mama say we do not know anything. I will not ask you things like that but I am thinking them. If anyone reads this letter my

Papa is a good man! Mama is trying to call him on her phone but no anser. Mama takes the pictures Olivier sent her to Ms. Defazio. We are very worryd about his arm and his face where he got hurt. Tell him we think about him all the time.

Bisous,

Anaïs

November 20

Dear Oma,

Well I make my report on our country to my class! Miss and the other students clap their hands at the end. Ms. Taylor comes too. I show my flag picture and was telling about our country and show pictures from the computer. There was question time at the end. Januel wants to know if there are tigers at my home. I say Januel I am sorry to say there are no tigers in my home. He looked a little sad. Why for goodness sake do I want a tiger in my home?

I tell my class about you. So much talking about you makes me wish I can be with you. I will take off my shoes and socks and walk on the brown dirt between the manioc and banana trees. I will see the women with their green black blue yellow purple dresses. I will sit in my tree house when it is hot and when it is cool I will come and drink tea with you under your tree. I will make a bookshelf for books and get a sofa to sit on so we can sit outside at night and look at the stars. It will be even better than the Halloween house!

Ms. Taylor said I did a very good report. So I am happy. But I am sad too. My report makes me miss my home and you and Olivier.

Bisous,

Anaïs

November 26

Dear Oma,

Today was the last day of school before we stay home for Thanksgiving. This is the American big holiday for the Pilgrims and for food. We have a short day today so we played games and are eating a lot of food. It was cool! Miss was bringing a salad and a pumpkin pie. It was so good I wanted to eat the hole thing! Ms. Taylor was bringing corn bread and applesauce. Many students bring food. We are eating and watching a movie. I love American holidays! They are so so fun!

Jenna and I made a card yesterday asking Mr. Dan to come to the party. This was our secret PLAN I was telling you about. And he did come! In between his work. Jenna got him food and I got Ms. Taylor. This is Mr. Dan I said. He speaks French! Ms. Taylor said they have met and she does not speak French. I looked at Jenna. Our PLAN was having a problem. But then I say Mr. Dan and I will teach you French! Now Ms. Taylor can say Bonjour ça va? and Au revoir. Jenna told Mr. Dan that Ms. Taylor made the applesauce. He said it was délicieux. Everyone knows what that means. Ms. Taylor had a big pretty smile on her face. Ha ha and Bingo! Our plan was at work. But then Mr. Dan put down his plate and said he had to go to work. Well it was only the first part of our PLAN. Jenna and I gave it a thumbs up.

Miss gave me food to take home to Mama. We love Thanksgiving! Happy Thanksgiving!

Bisous,

Anaïs

November 29

Dear Oma,

Vacations are so boring. There is nothing to do at the shelter and the family Potter is mad at the family Omar again. Mr. Potter say Mrs. Omar's cooking smells funny. The bad funny not the good funny. And Mr. Omar say the Potters sons leave the bisicles in the doorway and no one can walk by them. Then Mrs. Potter say the trash needs to go out. I miss school. I wonder if Mr. Dan is thinking of Ms. Taylor or if Ms. Taylor is thinking of Mr. Dan? I got one new idea. A good idea! I am thinking Ms. Taylor can ask Mr. Dan to tell us about his country and the way he came to America. He is like a Pilgrim too! I have a lot of time to think in the vacation. I can't wait to tell this idea to Jenna.

The best thing today was talking to you and Olivier on Monsieur's phone! It is so good to hear you talk! And we are happy Olivier says his arm is ok. Mama is very glad you are taking him back to the doctor. She asks to please let her know what he says.

Mama was taking me and Jean-Claude to the big library in the city today. I am happy to tell you it is the one good thing about America today! I love going to the library so so much. I was finding books and movies to take home to put into the tv at the shelter. For no money at all. Jean-Claude played a game on the computer so he was good. Mama talked to the library woman and she can take Jean-Claude to a French story time on Wednesday. We stayd a long time.

When we came out it was getting a little bit dark. Mama and Jean-Claude and me waited at the bus stop. I was looking at one of my new books. Jean-Claude said What is that? In French of course. I looked and was thinking it was only a little feather falling down. From a city bird. But then more white things were falling. What is this I said? Mama said it was snow. SNOW? Jean-Claude and I hear about snow but now it was hear and falling down! Jean-Claude tried to run and catch every one. Ha ha. It was funny. Mama had to hold him tite. Oma I have to tell you that snow is one very very beautiful and good thing about America today. There are hundreds thousands millions of tiny white pieces like flowers falling here and there and everywhere in the city. And when one falls on your face it is like a cold little baby kiss.

When we got home the snow was on the streets and

sidewalks. It was a little bit slippery but so white even in the dark. The bushes and trees lookd like they had little white hats. It snowed for a while. Snow makes the city quiet and sleepy. If you close your eyes right now I hope you will dream this beautiful picture of the sleepy white city.

Bisous,

Anaïs

December 4

Dear Oma,

Ok now I am tired of snow. Snow makes my sneakers wet and my feet cold. Snow is slippery. I slipped two times today at recess. And it was so white in the sun at recess that when I came inside I can not see anything. And it is cold! So cold! Cold colder coldest! The sun is shining but it is not doing a good job. And it gos to bed so so early now. I hope it is doing a good job at your home!

Mrs. F gave me a pair of snow boots today at school. They look like pillows on my feet but she says they will keep my feet warm. I think I will wear them all the time. She says she will look for a winter jacket for me too. And

I ask for one for Jean-Claude too. Now I know why the Pilgrims came to America with so many clothes! Somebody told them about winter! Nobody told me and Mama. What did the Native Americans do I am thinking with not many clothes? How did they live here in the winter? I hope somebody gave them snow boots.

Also today in school I have a problem with Miss. We have to write about the snow we are seeing. I was so happy to do this because snow is beautiful! I wanted to write that the snow looked like sugar on the bushes. Yes? Well do I know how to spell sugar? No for goodness sake because I am not a real American girl and American words are crazy! So I askt Miss. She said sugar was tricky. Yes another tricky thing! She said it is starting with a S. I write down a S. Then she said You and looked at me and is pointing to the paper. And I am thinking she is waiting for me to guess a letter and I say H? E? And she was saying You You pointing at my paper. So I was thinking I? O? And she was saying again You You You! Then she took my pencil from my hand and wrote a U. She and I were not happy one little bit. So now I can spell SUGAR but for goodness sake I do not know why YOU has to be the same as U!!!!!!

Ok now Halloween and Thanksgiving are finished

and we will learn about Christmas. I am happy because I know Christmas all ready and now I will not feel so STUPID! It is my holiday too! Joyeux Noël and Père Noël! Ha ha!

Mama says thank you for your card and the paper you sent! She will show the paper to Ms. Defazio so that it will help America to give us a silum. Mama was wishing maybe Papa and Olivier will be here soon but now she don't think so. We will miss them and you so much. But I am happy to tell you we are getting presents to send to you and Olivier. I cannot tell you what they are because it is a SECRET! We cannot send presents to Papa because we don't know where he is. I will give him so many presents when we see him again!

I know it is not Christmas yet but I will tell you and Olivier anyway—Joyeux Noël!

Bisous,

Anaïs

December 9

Dear Oma,

Ok I was so very very happy Christmas was coming because I know Christmas. Everything about Christmas

I think! But I do not. Christmas in America is red and green and Santa Cloz and Froste Snowman and Rudolf Reindeer and Tiny Tim. Do you know them? There are so many new things about Christmas here. Like jingle bells for goodness sake! I do not know jingle bells! And I am feeling stupid stupid STUPID again!

We also learn about other holidays. There is one called Hanika and one called Kwonza. Miss askt me and Ikran if we know Kwonza because she said it was a holiday in Africa. Africa? Really? Ikran and me don't know Kwonza. Do you know Kwonza? Is Kwonza in a small country somewhere? Miss was surprised. Kwonza is in Africa and I don't know it! I do not like the feeling that I am stupid! Again! Can I please tell you that I am starting to hate Christmas and Kwonza too? Is that a bad thing to say? I remember Christmas at home with you. That is the Christmas I want to have.

I am sorry to say but I cannot think of one good thing about America today.

Bisous,

Anaïs

December 13

Dear Oma,

Mama was taking Jean-Claude and me shopping today after school! We went to the BIG store called Goodwill. I love Goodwill! I got a dress that is soft and black on top. It is called velvet. And the bottom is white ruffles. That is what the lady at Goodwill called it. There are many pieces of white one after the other. At the top around my neck there are sparkles too. It is the most beautiful dress ever and Mama says I can wear it to church for Christmas. She says I can maybe wear it to school for my class Christmas party too. I love my new dress. It is the good, better, most beautiful best thing about America today!!!! I can't wait for Jenna and Ms. Taylor to see it.

We made Christmas cards today with Ms. Taylor. I made one for you, one for Papa, one for Olivier, one for Mama and Jean-Claude, one for Ms. Taylor and one for Mr. Dan. And one for Monsieur. You will not believe how beutiful they are and I was writing with my best kursiv writing too. Ms. Taylor was teaching Ikran and me how to make lists of all the things we will like to get for Christmas using COMMAS. Ikran wants to make friends, learn English. And she said a lot more in Somali but we didn't know what she said. I hope Ikran gets her present of learning English!

This is my list—Mama to get her papers so we can get a silum, Olivier to get better speshully his arm, Papa to be safe and to come to America, to see you in our country that is safe, lots of good food and Ms. Taylor and Mr. Dan to be good, better, best friends!!! But I didn't put this on my list for Ms. Taylor or she will see it. I also did not write the other thing I want. I want a home where we can stay for ever. A home with a sofa and books in the bookshelves and a million tiny lights like stars. A home like the Halloween house that is warm and happy for us. A home with a garden and a tree outside for birds to sit in. A home where we can stay together and make our own little bit of Africa in America. Maybe then I can be the real Anaïs in crazy America. Last night I dreamed so many dreams of Africa and America. I didn't wake up until I was all out of dreams.

Bisous,

Anaïs

December 18

Dear Oma,

Ha ha! It was one good day at my school today! Ms. Taylor was asking Mr. Dan to come tell me and Ikran about his trip to America. Jenna and Januel were mad they didn't come.

Mr. Dan is so so nice. If I was Ms. Taylor I will like him so so much! He was wearing his good clothes and looked very nice. Jenna told me a word for him is HANDSOME! He was bringing pictures of his country. It is Libya. It is in Africa but way up top. His cousin is a taxi driver here in the city. That is why he came here and the person he lives with. He speaks Arabic, French and Italian. He is learning English. He was teaching languages in high school in Libya. He hopes he will be a teacher in America some day. He goes to school at night. He talked about Libya and the way he got to America. He's funny and tells jokes. One time he was in a boat with many many other people and it started to go down in the ocean but it didn't. He made it sound easy. But I don't think getting to America is ever easy.

He showed us on the map where he worked to make money to get to America. He said the country looked like a boot! He had dictionaries with him and we used the computer to translate some words. Mr. Dan and Ms. Taylor were both of them smiling a lot and laughing because our words were all mixed up in English, French, Italian, Arabic, Spanish and, for sure, some Somali. At recess I told Jenna our PLAN was really really working so good! Ikran nodded and gave it a thumbs up too but I don't know if she understands.

It was a very good day. I am still smiling and hope you will smile, too, when you see my letter!

Bisous,

Anaïs

December 21

Dear Oma,

Ok school is no good. Remember my most beautiful new dress that Mama say I can wear to school for the Christmas party? Well Miss say today we are having PAJAMA DAY tomorrow. The class yelled YAY!!!! What for goodness sake is Pajama Day I ask Jenna? Jenna tells me everyone wears pajamas and brings a stuffed animal and we lie on the floor and watch movies and eat food. But I want to wear my beautiful dress I say! You can't say Jenna. I don't want to wear pajamas I say. You're crazy she say! And she goes and tells Brittany and Januel what I say and they laff.

So I tell Mama no beautiful black velvet dress with white ruffles and sparkles. Pajamas. Pajamas she say? She say I cannot wear pajamas to school. No way. I don't want to wear pajamas but all the other students will wear them I say! She get mad and I get mad. She say I cannot wear my old pajamas and she don't have money to go get new ones tonight for goodness sake! School is no good and I hate American Christmas and I hate Frostie and Rudolf and stupid cande kanz too! I

want my old Christmas with Père Noël and beautiful
dresses!!!

You and Mama don't know how HARD AMERICA
is. Or COLD. Or CRAZY! I DON'T KNOW WHY
YOU AND MAMA MAKE US COME HERE. I DON'T
HAVE MY FRIENDS FROM HOME. The food is NO
GOOD. NO STARS LIKE HOME only maybe one
maybe two and clouds. Lots and lots of CLOUDS ALL
THE TIME. And No Papa and Olivier!

I WANT TO GO HOME! PLEASE OMA! Tell Mama
I have to COME HOME AND LIVE WITH YOU!

Ok so Mama see my letter to you. She say we talk
when Jean-Claude is asleep. When he is in bed Mama
makes us tea and tells me this story. She tells me that she
and Papa have to sell their house for us to get money to
come here. I know that. But then Mama say she really
wants us to come to America but they still don't have
the money. Mama say you really want us to come to
America. I know that too. But she say do I know why? I
say to get somewhere safe. But she says there is another
why. The most important why of all. It is so me and
Jean-Claude can go to school and have a good life. A
good, better, best life. That is the most important why

of all. And because of this most important why of all Mama say you have to sell your house and your land to the husband of Monsieur's daughter to get more money for us to come to America. And you ask your cousins and sisters and brothers and everybody for money to get us to America. And you and Mama get enuf money for Mama and me and Jean-Claude. Olivier say he wants to stay with you and go to school and try to help Papa. And Papa cannot get a visa because the soldiers are looking for him. But I hope hope hope Papa and Olivier can come some day. So Mama tell me you have no home now so that we can have a home.

Oma, why you never tell me this! Mama say you don't want me to be sad but now I am missing you and your home and your tree and your garden more and more than ever. And Mama and me cry cry cry together. But when we stop crying Mama say there is one good thing. What I say? And she tell me that you are living with Monsieur now because you have liked each other for a long time! Another thing I did not know!

Oma, I hope you are very happy for sure. And Monsieur too. And I will try to be a good girl and go to school and help Mama. But living in America is not easy. No way. And I don't always do things the way Mama wants and it is not easy taking care of Jean-Claude for goodness sake! And it is not easy in school. No way. But I will try. Sometimes I think of the Pilgrims and Mr. Dan coming in the small boats. We are all trying to live in Crazy America! I only wish Crazy America was not so so so far from you.

Bisous,

Anaïs

December 22

Dear Oma,

We got a card from Olivier today! We are all very happy to see his writing and hear he is feeling better. It is good he can write with his good arm. He say he will send another picture of his arm in the bandage still. Tell him thank you and I will write to him soon. Tell him we miss him a lot. Tell him I hope he can come to America soon. I am thinking it will be nice to have a big brother again.

Mama showed your paper to Ms. Defazio and she says it will help us stay. Ms. Defazio told Mama to get as many papers or pictures as possible. Mama will call you about it.

So today was the last day of school. Instead of my most beautiful black and white velvet dress with ruffles and sparkles I wore my old school clothes. Miss was bringing extra robes and stuffed animals for any student. I picked out a robe. It had hairs on it from Miss's cat. And I picked out a stuffd rabbit. Ikran pickd a bear. It looked a lot like her. She wasn't wearing pajamas too. Jenna and some others brought blankets for the floor. It looked a little bit like the shelter to me. Januel wore superhero pajamas and ran around stepping on people. Even Miss was wearing pink pajamas for goodness sake! We watched a funny movie and ate popcorn. When there was a kiss the whole class made a loud noise like old hippopotames in the river.

So now we are at home. Mama is washing the dishes in the kitchen then she will make us some tea. I was reading a story to Jean-Claude. It is a funny book with numbers. Then Jean-Claude likes it when I count his toes. It is the song Monsieur was teaching us at school. One Little Two Little Three Little. I teach Jean-Claude how to count in English. I tell him how fun numbers are. We count everything in our room. I hope he will go to sleep soon.

Then Mama and I have our tea. And look at our

Christmas tree. We have a real one in our room! Jenna's father was getting one for them and got one for us too! It was a big and very good surprise! The shelter people didn't know if it was safe but Jenna's father talked to them and it's now ok. They were bringing us two long strings of colored lights too.

Mama and I put them on the tree. Jean-Claude was no help for sure. Here is my one good thing about America today. The room is a little bit dark but the lights make pretty colors and shadows of the tree branches on the walls. Like feathers. I am lying under the tree and looking up. I can see so many many branches with tiny colored lights in them. They are like the stars in the Halloween house! Not real stars but beautiful anyway. I hope you are looking at the real stars tonight and that they are smiling down and taking care of you.

Also, on the tree are our Christmas cards, the one from Olivier, one from me to Mama and Jean-Claude, one from Jenna, one from you and Monsieur, one from Ms. Taylor and one from Mr. Dan in French! We are looking every day for a card from Papa.

I hope when you get my letter you will see me under the tree and smile. I want in all my heart for

you to smile and be happy, happyer, happyest at this
Christmas! I love you very much! Joyeux Noël!! And
to Monsieur too!!

Bisous,

Anaïs

December 27

Dear Oma,

We have been very busy! But I hope you had a good,
very great Christmas with Olivier and Monsieur! Did
you hear anything about Papa? We went to church and
I got to wear my new beautiful black and white dress.
There was a dinner at church too with lots of food and
our church friends. Then we had presents at home.
Jean-Claude got a new robot toy and some crayons from
Santa Clouz. I got another new dress. A very beautiful
blue one! And I got three books and things for painting!

Then Jenna called and said she wanted to take us
sleding! I was not knowing very much about sleding
but I said yes thank you yes you are very welcome to
take us sleding any time you want! So Jenna's Mama and

Mama talked on the phone and we went sleding today! I was thinking Jean-Claude would get wet or cold or cry for no reason but he did not. It was so so fun! Jenna's parents came in their van and we all got in. We went to a park where there is a hill. It is close to the ocean too so you can sled and watch boats at the same time! COOL!!!

We took turns because there were two sleds and six people. Jenna has a big brother but he was some other place with friends. We went sleding again and again. Jenna and I went together. I was so scared at first. It felt like I was falling and I screamed STOP STOP! Jenna laffed and we stopped. After that I wasn't scared again but my inside was still a little bit scared when we went fast. Jenna's Mama wanted to take Jean-Claude but he said no no. I took him with me. He laffed and laffed. He liked rolling down the hill too. Mama did not go until the last time. I got her to go sleding with me one time. She held me tite and screamed. But it was a good scream. She was smiling and laffing so I know it was a good scream. It was such a fun fun day. Jenna's Mama took a picture. I will send it to you so you can see your American sleding Mama Jean-Claude and me! Then we even had hot chocolate in the van in the parking lot. Americans like hot chocolate milk in winter. Hot chocolate and sleding are TWO very good things about America today!

Did you get the presents from us?

Bisous,

Anaïs

January 1

Dear Oma,

Bonne Année!! Happy New Year! Thank you so much for your phone call today! I love talking to you on the phone! I am glad you are happy living with Monsieur and glad he will take care of you! I am glad he likes having Olivier there too. I like telling you about our Christmas tree. And you say too the lites on our tree are like the stars. I like when you say the stars are always there even if we cannot see them. I will try to remember that even if we have stupid clouds like we do right now!

I am writing also to say thank you for the beautiful notebook and pen you gave to me. They came in the mail yesterday. And I see you put cloth on the notebook.

It looks like one of your dresses. It is very beautiful and looks and feels like a little bit of you. Thank you so so much!

I don't have much to say. Americans don't do the speshel things for the New Year like we do at home. Mama let me stay up watching movies until the New Year came. I was watching from our window waiting for everyone to go into the street to say Happy New Year! Happy New Year! But no one did. We were hearing a few fireworks but then it was all quiet again. No people, no Happy New Years and no stars because of clouds. It didn't feel like the New Year at all. I am missing the New Year at home. Write and tell me what it was like for you.

It is snowing again and cold. Mama makes us stay inside. We went to the library yesterday and got more movies. I can't wait for school again.

On the way home from the library we saw a big box on the sidewalk. Jean-Claude wanted to look inside but Mama pulled him away. Then I saw two legs. Mama I said? She told me sometimes if people don't have a home they stay in big boxes. I don't believe her. But I saw the two legs with my eyes. I did not know some people in America have no home. I was thinking everyone had a home. We have a home in the shelter. Why don't the people go to a motel or a shelter? Why does someone live in a box?

I walk home thinking you said to me there is a home waiting for us somewhere. We just have to find it. Please say a prayer that we will find it.

I am so glad Olivier is with you. I know you take good care of him. I hope the soldiers never never come back. I hope Papa is somewhere safe. I know I cannot ask you about him and you cannot say anything. We did not get a card or phone call from Papa. Mama does not say but she has worrying in her eyes. I wish the soldiers and the mining company will know what a good man Papa is.

I have to go and play with Jean-Claude while Mama cooks. We are drawing pictures of us and our Christmas tree and putting them with this letter for you. The picture of the pretty Christmas tree is by me. The other one is by Jean-Claude.

Bisous and in American XOXO,

Anaïs

January 3

Dear Oma,

Mama talked to Papa today! But we do not know where he is. He called to say he is ok. He say there was some fighting. He can not tell if the fighters are the government soldiers or rebels. Papa wants Olivier to stay with you and go to school. He doesn't want Olivier to look for him. Mama is worried if the soldiers come back again and hurt Olivier or you or Monsieur. Mama had not talked to Papa for a long time. She wants him and Olivier to try to get to the US someway. Papa don't know what will happen.

She was trying to call you but it was too late. She will try tomorrow.

We sit in our room tonight drinking our sad tea. Mama and I feel like we are very very far away.

We hope you and Monsieur and Olivier are happy and safe.

Bisous,

Anaïs

January 6

Dear Oma,

Happy Three Kings Day! We did not do anything speshul but Mama cooked us a good dinner. And we were thinking about you and Olivier and Papa. And Monsieur. It was time to put the Christmas tree outside. Its tiny leaves were falling falling everywhere. I try to sweep them but then I see one more one more! But the good thing is I take the colored lights and put them up around our windows so now we have little colored lights all the time! I think they look like little stars so we have them even when it is cloudy. Not the real stars but almost. I hope you have the real stars smiling down on you tonight!

    I can't wait for school to start tomorrow!

                Bisous,

                Anaïs

January 7

Dear Oma,

YAY! I was so happy to go back to school today but I am

sorry to say there is a new student in my class. His name is Hassan. Miss moved our desks. Hassan's desk is next to my desk and Jenna sits next to Brittany now. Hassan does not know English. He was looking with big eyes maybe the way I was looking on my first day. He had a red soccer shirt. It looked very new but cold because of short sleeves. Mrs. F took him to get a jacket and a backpack. Hassan came back with a pink backpack with a soccer ball on it. I am thinking what is he doing? He does not know anything about American schools!

Ok Hassan I say. Take my backpack and give me the pink one. He likes the soccer ball one. Trust me I say. He don't know what I say but he sees the other boys and their backpacks and then takes mine. The black one with the yellow and black bird. I will get it back from him someday.

Ok Hassan I SAY. Take my Backpack & give ME THE pink one. Trust me I SAY

Hassan speaks only Arabic. No one knows what he says. Ikran speaks Somali but she don't know what he say too. When it is time to go to Ms. Taylor we take him. Ikran wants to take care of him like one of her little brothers but Hassan does not want a little mama.

I was happy to go to Ms. Taylor. I had not seen her for two weeks! She said hello to Hassan and said she was thinking Mr. Dan knows Arabic. She called the office and Mr. Dan came to help. Yay Mr. Dan! Hassan was speaking Arabic to Mr. Dan then Mr. Dan was speaking the words to me in French then I was speaking in English to Ms. Taylor. Ikran was for sure speaking Somali.

So this is how we learnd Hassan comes from Iraq. We lookd at the map but Hassan did not find his city. Hassan told Mr. Dan his family had a big house and he likes to play soccer. And he has a mama and a papa and two little sisters and a little baby brother. And he says his school was only for boys. He askt if Mr. Dan will be his teacher but Mr. Dan said no. His job was to clean the school and fix things. Ms. Taylor and Miss are his teachers. Hassan did not look happy.

Ms. Taylor askt Mr. Dan to tell Hassan we will talk about what we did for the vacation. Then Mr. Dan had to go. Ms. Taylor made us write about it and draw a picture. I said she can write about her vacation too and draw a picture! I was sad to see Mr. Dan was not in her picture but maybe I said to Jenna at recess she was thinking about him anyway! Hassan didn't draw any picture. He was writing his name but it was taking a long time. Ms. Taylor helped him. She also asked him to write his name in Arabic. It looked like spaghetti to me.

We are going to start learning about the Arctic and the Antarctic with Miss. I am sorry to say they are places with a lot of snow. Learning about more SNOW for goodness sake! Really? I said to Miss that if we learned about AFRICA it will be nice and warm.

When I got on the bus to go home Hassan got on too! He is living in the shelter on some other floor. No one told me! His mama was there to get him at the bus stop. She was so happy to see him but he did not look happy to see her. Not one bit. I think maybe he was looking like me when I got home from my number one day at school.

When I got home there was good news. Mama says we will get a new apartment! So maybe I will not be here with Hassan for much time. Mama will see it tomorrow.

We are hoping it will be the one good thing about America today!

Bisous and xoxoxo!

Anaïs

January 9

Dear Oma,

I do not know what to say. I do not know so many words in English to say it. Mama did not see the new apartment until today. She went to see it when I was in school. She said it is very nice and is not a lot of money but is in a part of the city that is not so good. She saw one old man neighbor. She said the building did not smell good. But the most bad part of all is that I will have to go to another school! The apartment is not in the part of the city where my school is! What can I say to Mama? I know she wants an apartment for us with rooms and a kitchen and a place for Papa and Olivier to come. I want a new home too but I do not want to leave my school. No no no way! I will have to leave Ms. Taylor, Mr. Dan, Jenna, Ikran, Miss, even Januel! Can I say this to Mama? I think there are maybe tears in my

eyes and she was seeing them. I try to hide them. I don't
know what to say.

Please say a prayer that something good will come
for us. And I will say a prayer for you tonight, too.

Bisous,

Anaïs

January 11

Dear Oma,

If you said a prayer for us I think it was the right one!
Bingo, Oma! Because we are not moving to the new
apartment! Mama talked to many people and she learnd
it was not a good place. So we will stay at the shelter
for longer and I can go to my school! I am so happy! I
am even thinking the shelter is one good thing about
America today!

Today in school I learned something about the
Arctic that is a little bit crazy. Maybe a very big crazy!
We learned about animals in the Arctic that are brown
in the summer and in the winter they turn white! Is
this true you say? Am I telling you a story? Miss says it
is very true! These animals they have fur that is brown.

But in the winter these animals turn their fur to white so they look like the snow! Crazy? I think so! And this happens every summer and winter. I know because I asked Miss even though Januel laffed at me.

I was not saying anything more but I am thinking brown, white, white, brown, all the time. When I go to Ms. Taylor I have to say, Ms. Taylor what is this thing about animals changing from brown to white and white to brown? And before she can say anything I say what will happen to me? It is winter and I am brown! You are brown! I am thinking what will Mama say if some day I go home and I am starting to turn white? I am thinking maybe this is some terrible sickness thing that happens in America and nobody was telling us!

Ms. Taylor takes my hand in her very beautiful brown hand and tells me not to worry about it at all. Not one bit. I will not be turning to white. It is only the stupid, or not stupid, animals in the Arctic. They need to do it to live she says. We can live just fine she says the way we are. Are you sure I say? Yes she says she is sure. Then she asks me and Ikran and Hassan if we will want to turn white? Ikran and Hassan don't understand. But me I was never thinking that way before. Ms. Taylor gets out a mirror and we look in it. I don't think I will be me if I was white. Ms. Taylor tells me I am so beautiful. She tells Ikran she is beautiful and Ikran is happy. She tells Hassan he is handsome but he does not look happy or maybe he don't understand.

But it was fun looking in the mirror. One two three four of us. Each brown a little bit different. Ms. Taylor talked about our COOL and beautiful browns. That's what Ms. Taylor said anyway. I love Ms. Taylor! She is one good thing about America today for sure!

Bisous,

Anaïs

January 15

Dear Oma,

I am not a happy girl today. Not one little bit! Because today Miss picked Hassan's name out of the hat and now he is Student of the Week and we have to write letters to him. Hassan didn't understand and looked scared but then Mr. Dan came and told him what Student of the Week is. Now Hassan thinks this makes him the most important person ever! He took my eraser today and was throwing it up and down. The other boys were laffing. I had to take it back from him. Jenna thinks he is funny sometimes.

At recess the girls were playing the game called hopscotch in America. I was telling them we have that game in my country, too! Today we made the game on the snow and used a snowball to play it. Hassan kicked a ball through the hopscotch game and I yelled at him to stop but then he slipped and fell. Hassan has brand new sneakers and is not used to the snow. It was very funny! Hassan got very mad and pushed me over. So I pushed him back. The recess lady took us to the office and I had to write a sorry letter to the Principal. Hassan had to write a letter too but I don't know what it said because he can only write in Arabic!

In the afternoon I went to Ms. Taylor with Ikran and Hassan. We were still mad. Mr. Dan came to help and we all talked in our languages. Hassan didn't say much but there was some words about it is better if girls stay away from the boys. Ha ha! Really I said? I told Ms. Taylor what happened. Ikran talked a lot, too. It was something about the recess because she got up and showed us hopscotch and pushing. But we don't know what she said. Ms. Taylor says we are all friends at school. Maybe if she says it many many more times it will be true. Ha ha!

And then we had to write our letters to Student of the Week Hassan. Hassan worked on writing his name and abcs with Ms. Taylor while Ikran and I tried to write our letters. I am happy to say the bell rang before we had to do it. Maybe I will give Hassan back his pink backpack. Ha!

Bisous,

Anaïs

January 19

Dear Oma,
I am very tired tonight. School is hard. Mostly because I had to do the final draft of my letter to Stupid Student of the Week Hassan today. Here is my letter.

Dear Hassan,
I can see you like recess and playing on the playground. You are good at running and you like soccer. Maybe you will be on a soccer team

someday. You like to laugh too. I think it is good to laugh. Maybe someday you will tell a funny joke in class?

After this Ms. Taylor and I could not think of anything else to say. She is very smart at finding words that are easy and don't say much! I love Ms. Taylor!!!! We don't get our Student of the Week letters till the end of the year so Hassan can not get this letter and get mad at me for a long long time. Ha ha.

Mama says she talked to you on the phone today while I was at school. She said you had not been hearing anything from Papa. We have not too. We pray for him every night. For you and Olivier and Monsieur too.

Bisous,

Anaïs

January 24

Dear Oma,

Winter is still here. Miss say to me that at my home in Africa I am having summer! She say when we have winter you get summer and when we get summer you get winter. But I tell her it is the rainy season now in my country. A lot of rain for January and February. She was thinking you are having summer now.

I think about the rain at home and about Papa. Where is he? Is he finding a place where it is safe and dry? I know I cannot write very much about him. But I don't know where he is. I wish so so much that I can put him and you and Olivier and maybe even Monsieur on a plane and get you here.

If you were here you can see the snow! We have so much snow you will not believe it. In America people make a man out of snow! We will take you to the park and you can help us make a snowman. Jenna says she makes big balls out of snow. We will make one two three big balls. We will put rocks to make the eyes and a carrot for the nose. Then a hat and a scarf and branches from the tree for the arms. It will be so fun if you are here and helping us make a snowman! Then we will sit on a bench and look at the oshun and drink the hot chocolate. Oma, I wish wish wish I can make it be true!

Jean-Claude is drawing a picture of a snowman that I will put in this letter. I am telling you it is a snowman because it looks like the potatos we had last night for dinner. I take Jean-Claude to the kitchen and we find a cup and I show him how we can put the cup on paper and draw circles around it with a pencil. Jean-Claude is trying to draw a new snowman now with real circles.

We are finishing our Arctic and Antarctic projects this week. I am writing about penguins because they are so cute. Do you know penguins? They are funny black and white birds. They stay black and white all the time and do not change colors. I think they must be CRAZY because they like to play on the snow and swim in the ice cold water but I like them anyway.

Ms. Taylor is helping me with my penguin project. I have to read it to the class soon. I saw Mr. Dan in the hall and told him about penguins and showed him my pictures. He knows a lot more about penguins now. I got a good idea to ask him to come to Ms. Taylor's room to hear me practice reading it. He said he will be happy to come. Ha ha. Sometime I feel very smart! I will tell you more in my next letter.

Bisous,

Anaïs

January 28

Dear Oma,

I had so much fun today! In the morning I mean. Mr.
Dan came to Ms. Taylor's room and sat in a chair and
listend while I read my report on Penguins. He said it
was very good. He asked a few questions about words
he didn't know. Like Nest and Huddle and Webbed
Feet. He and Ms. Taylor talked for a little bit and looked
at the maps in my project. Ikran read her report on
Lemmings. Ikran likes the lemmings even though
every animal eats them! Miss calls them Arctic Nachos.
This is an American snack like chips. But Ikran says
they are cute and pats them in the pictures she makes.
Hassan pick the Killer Whale. He pretends to eat all the
lemmings and penguins.

 In the afternoon I gave my report to my class.
They liked it and we talked about the other reports on
penguins, too. It was good until the bus ride home.
Hassan was sitting on the other side of the bus and
kept laffing and saying something to me. I was saying
What? What? He got mad. Then I see he was trying to
say Killer Whale Killer Whale and looking like he was

eating a penguin but it sounded like Keelr Wall Keelr Wall. I was laffing laffing. Hassan was so mad he jumpd off the bus at the shelter and ran right past his smiling mama. Hassan is annoying but funny sometimes too!

Bisous,

Anaïs

February 6

Dear Oma,

School is not good and not bad. There is still snow and it is cold and dark like night when Mama wake me and Jean-Claude up in the morning. I wish there are stars to make the night look more friendly.

The one good thing about school is going to see Ms. Taylor. Ikran and me are writing about what makes a good frend because we are getting ready for Valentines Day! Soon we will make valentines cards. Ha ha, I hope you will like the one I will make for you! Hassan is working on making words and reading them. He is not happy we can do more than him.

We are also making a card for Ms. Taylor. It is a SECRET. Ikran and me work on it in our regular class.

And then I have an idea! We can make a card for Ms.
Taylor and say it is from Mr. Dan! And maybe we can
also give one to Mr. Dan and say it is from Ms. Taylor! I
think maybe Ikran was understanding me. For goodness
sake what a PLAN! We have a lot of work to do but it
will be so, so fun! I tell Jenna. Yay for our new PLAN!

Miss sent home a letter to Mama and all the parents
today saying each student will give valentines cards
to all the students. This means I have to give one to
Hassan. I am not happy but then I think he will not be
happy having to give one to me too. Ha ha!

Bisous,

Anais

February 11

Dear Oma,

Did you know chocolate comes from Africa? Ms. Taylor
was reading facts about Valentines to Ikran and me and
Hassan and we learned chocolate comes from Africa.
Wow I said! Chocolate is one very good thing that
everyone LOVES and it comes from Africa. Ms. Taylor
loves chocolate too and she said she will bring some
chocolate to us on Valentines Day!

Ms. Taylor helped us write our names many many times on valentines cards today for our class. She gave cards for us to use. I picked the ones with robots, Ikran picked the ones with little baby dogs, and Hassan picked the ones with soccer balls. Hassan did not finish writing his name on his cards so Ms. Taylor asked me to help him at the shelter tonight. I am NOT HAPPY but said ok. I only do this because Ms. Taylor asks me.

So Hassan came to our room. Jean-Claude thinks Hassan is the best thing in the world! Mama put Jean-Claude to bed and now the three of us are sitting at the table. Mama gave us hot chocolate. Chocolate from Africa! I am writing to you and Hassan is writing his name on his cards. It is very hard for him I think but he is doing better. I tell him Good Job.

Tomorrow Ikran and I have more work to do on the SECRET cards for Ms. Taylor and Mr. Dan. I learnd some Valentines cards don't need names on them so we can give one to Ms. Taylor and one to Mr. Dan and not say who they are from. But me and Ikran hope they will think they make them for each other! We are using fancy red and white papers and glitter from Ms.

Taylor's room and we are drawing hearts and flowers with markers. I'm hoping Ikran understands this plan. I never know what she knows and what she don't know. But for me it is EXCITING!

MAKING CARDS & WRITING LETTERS

And I made a card for you of course and one for Papa and one for Olivier. I wish somehow Papa will know I love him even if he does not get the card. Mama mailed them today. I don't know where she mailed Papa's card to. I hope you get your card for Valentines Day. I love you!

XOXO!

Anaïs

February 15

Dear Oma,

Well you will never think what happened but I got sick and did not go to school for Valentines Day! My head hurt. My inside and my outside. Every bit of me. I stayed in my bed and was sleeping a long time. Mama stayed home from her English class and made tea and made Jean-Claude to be quiet. But I was so sad I was missing Valentines Day! We had a great PLAN and now I was thinking the secret plan for Ms. Taylor and Mr. Dan will not ever happen. It made me feel even more sicker.

But today I was feeling much better so I went to school and you will never guess. Ms. Taylor was smiling so much when I saw her and she saved chocolate for me too. She thanked me for my card and said she got another card too. Because Ikran gave it to her and said it was from Mr. Dan! Ikran was knowing what to do! YAY FOR IKRAN!! Ikran said with her words and with her hands that she gave the other card to Mr. Dan and told him it was from Ms. Taylor. I saw Mr. Dan in the hall. He was smiling a lot and laffing a little bit too. I hope our plan is working. They both look happy. Do you think they know we made the cards? I was so surprised that Ikran made our VALENTINE PLAN WORK!

We had our chocolate with Ms. Taylor. Chocolate is the one good thing about America today but also because it comes from Africa! Ms. Taylor told us to close our eyes and think if we can feel something from our old homes. I closed my eyes and was thinking of things that are good and brown like chocolate. I think when I was waiting on the road for Papa to come home from the mine and then seeing his brown face walking to me. I see the little brown path to your door and the wooden steps to my treehouse and the tea I have with you that you make from plants. Then I remember you are at Monsieur's house. Well the chocolate was good but if I can wish it I will want to be really with you. Writing a letter is ok but I think a hug in your brown arms will be much better.

I will ask Mama if we can send you and Olivier and Monsieur some American chocolate from Africa.

Bisous,

Anaïs

February 17

Dear Oma,

I have something to write about Papa. Maybe you know it all ready? Maybe not. Mama was trying to call you but the phone was not working. She say sorry so I write anyway.

Papa called to say the soldiers came close to where he was and almost were finding him. His friend helped him get away in time. He says he is thinking of taking the papers about the mining company to the newspaper but it is dangerous. Mama tells me the mining company is the company of our president's brother and they are keeping the money from the mine instead of giving it to the country. I ask Mama if it's ok to say this in my letter but she say Papa is already in trouble. And it is the truth. The money from the mine is to help our country she says and not just one or two people. Papa is afraid of the soldiers coming back to hurt you and Olivier and even Monsieur now. Oma, I am afraid the soldiers will find Papa. And he cannot run fast with his bad leg. And I am afraid they will come to Monsieur's house.

Mama and I hope and pray you and Olivier and
Monsieur are safe. We will try to call you soon.

We love you. Bisous,

Anaïs

February 21

Dear Oma,

I am happy and sad and worrying too all the same time.
Papa just called to tell us he went to your house to get
Olivier because he was afraid the soldiers will come
back to take him away because they are mad at Papa. He
say sometimes they take boys to work in the mine and
Olivier's arm is still not good. Now he and Olivier are
hiding and trying to get somewhere safe. Mama and me
worry about you and Monsieur but Papa say he thinks
you will be ok. He is glad Monsieur's cousin is in the
government and can help you. We think of you every
minute.

I think I will paint a picture for you with the
painting things I got for Christmas. To make me and
you feel better. To help take the worrying away. When it
is dry I will put it in this letter and mail it to you. I think

I will paint a sunny day for you and a garden you will love. Are the rains stopping? Are you going to plant new seeds in Monsieur's garden?

I cannot think of anything else to write. Jenna's cousins are at her house so I'm thinking we will not go sledding with her in the vacation this time. The snow is not as good as it was any how.

I will go paint for you now. I will not look at the cloudy day outside but only at the sunny day on my paper.

Bisous,

Anaïs

February 24

Dear Oma,

Thank you a hundred million times for your letter! And thank Monsieur for writing it. Mama and me and Jean-Claude too are so so happy to hear you are ok. I am glad you are thinking of planting seeds in Monsieur's garden.

We still have not talked to Papa or Olivier. Mama was talking to a woman in her English class and the woman told her there is some fighting. But we don't know if Papa and Olivier are in those places or not.

I can see Mama is worrying. I am making her some tea. I don't know what else to do. There is a pain in my heart but I don't know where to put it.

I have to go now and help Hassan with his homework because Ms. Taylor askt me to do it. Hassan is funny. At school he looks like he does not know me when other boys are around. But at the shelter he comes and gets help from me. I think he likes sitting with Mama and me where it is quiet. Maybe he is hoping I will do his homework for him. Ha ha. Surprise! No I will not!

Mama says to you don't worry about Olivier. Papa will keep him safe now. We want you only to worry about you and Monsieur keeping safe.

Bisous,

Anaïs

February 27

Dear Oma,

We are not hearing anything from Papa and Olivier. If we do we will call you right away. And if you hear anything you can please call us?

Here is something to make you happy. At school there are some times when Mama has to come to the school and talk to Miss and Ms. Taylor. The times are called confernses. They talk about what I am learning. I want them to say I am learning a lot of good English! But some days I feel like I am learning nothing. Like I am stupid like a baby.

So Mama and Jean-Claude come to my school today. I didn't take the bus home to the shelter but I waited for them at school. There were other mothers and fathers waiting in the hall for other teachers too. I was hoping Mama was not going to look very different from the other mothers. And I was hoping Jean-Claude was not going to be annoying. But then I saw Januel with his Mama. His Mama was nice and talked to my Mama. She even knows a little French.

Miss was happy to see Mama. And a man came who could speak English and French too! He told Mama everything that Miss said but in French. I learned a lot about what my class has been doing in school! And he told Miss everything that Mama said but in English. Miss was telling Mama that I am so so good in math! Yay! I am working on my times tables but Mama knows that because I tell her. Miss show Mama my math work.

Jean-Claude was sitting with Mama wanting to play in the room but Mama was holding on to him very tite. He was not looking at my beautiful numbers and kursiv writing.

Then we went to see Ms. Taylor with the man who could speak French. Ms. Taylor was very nice and smiled and told Mama I was doing a good job. A good, better, best job! The man said everything in French to Mama. I was listening and suddenly was thinking I don't know some of the words he is saying. Maybe I am forgetting French? I don't want to forget French! Maybe I will ask Mr. Dan if I will forget French if I learn more English.

No matter what will happen I will always remember one word in French for you,

Bisous,

Anaïs

March 1

Dear Oma,
You remember the painting things I got for Christmas? So I was happy when we were getting to use the painting

things in art class today. We learned to keep the colors clean with water and only mix the colors on the mixing place. I know some of this already. Then the art teacher showd us how to blend colors together to make new colors. That was the new word for today. BLEND. It was so fun to make the blue and yellow turn green. We all made different greens! Then we put red and blue together to make purple and then red and yellow to make orange. But brown is the hardest color to make. You have to mix red, yellow and blue the rite way to make a brown. Did you know some colors make new colors? It was so cool!

I was telling Ms. Taylor it is very hard to make brown. So she got out her paints and we made lots of browns or sometimes purples or sometimes blacks. It took a long time but was fun. Ikran and Hassan and me learned to make really good browns.

And Ms. Taylor was talking about blends and beautiful browns. Warm browns, soft browns, dark browns, loud browns, sweet browns. She told us we are so lucky to be a blend of colors. She put out her arm and I did too and Ikran and even a little slow Hassan did too. And guess what! Mr. Dan was in the hall cleaning. Ms. Taylor called to him and he came in.

Ms. Taylor was trying to explain to Mr. Dan and I

helped in French. Maybe he thought we were crazy. I know Hassan was thinking she was crazy. Anyway we put our five arms on the table. They were five different brown blends for sure! Ms. Taylor showed us a piece of white paper. She said she will much rather be a blend of colors than have no color like the white paper. Mr. Dan said it too. Absolument. Ms. Taylor and Mr. Dan are the two good things about America today for sure for sure!!! And I have to say that Ms. Taylor's arm looked very beautiful next to Mr. Dan's arm!

Anyway it was a good day.

Bisous,

Anaïs

March 3

Dear Oma,

Do you hear from Papa or Olivier? We do not and Mama and me are worryed. Mama asks her friends here and is trying to call Papa's friends. We think about you and Monsieur too. Please write or call and tell us you are ok.

Winter is not wanting to leave but I wish it will

hurry up. Miss says Spring is her favorite time of the year. She says it is beautiful. She say everything, even the whole world, will turn green! Green? Really? In crazy America the whole world turns green? For goodness sake, I only want winter to go someplace else.

A funny thing happened at school today. Not good or bad funny. Just funny. Mrs. F came to our classroom. She was the teacher who was teaching us about PERSONAL SPACE because the little fish likes to be alone. Today she was teaching us about COMMUNICATION which is about being careful with the words you are saying. And she made us play a game. We stood in a long line and she told the first person something and that person said it in whispering to the next person and on and on. So I didn't hear the word and didn't know what to say and for sure Ikran and Hassan didn't too. Hassan was trying to look like the other boys and look cool and smart. Mrs. F was saying Just Say What You Hear. It was all blah blah blah to me. At the end of the game Mrs. F said to everyone the words are Ketchup Is Very Tasty On An Ice Cream Sandwich!!!!

The one good thing was that Mrs. F said to everyone Now You Can See How Important Communication Is And We Need To Speak Carefully And Clearly And

ICE CREAM *sandwich*!

How Hard It Is To Hear Sometimes Especially For Annie and Ikran and Hassan. But she forgot to say it is also a good thing if you know English.

Bisous,

Anaïs

March 6

Dear Oma,

Olivier called today! I was at school when he called so I am sad I did not hear him. Mama said he and Papa are ok and they are safe! That is all we know. But we are so happy! Mama is smiling and singing while she cooks dinner. She calld her friends to tell them. Jean-Claude and I are drawing pictures of Olivier and Papa. Everyone in the pictures has smilie faces.

Maybe winter is thinking of leaving. The snow is not

so much and there is more sun for more time in the day. But the world has not turned green the way Miss says it will. I am a little bit afraid of what a green world will be like but Miss says it is great. Are you working in Monsieur's garden? I think he will be happy to have you doing it!

Mama says people are telling her there are more apartments in the spring. She is hoping she can find one soon. I know she wishes Papa and Olivier will be in the new apartment too. An apartment for us will be good but I am afraid I will maybe have to go to a new school. I am tired of new. I want old.

Like my American school! It feels like old to me now. Yesterday I was so so happy to go to Ms. Taylor's room and I saw her eating her lunch. She told me Mr. Dan had given it to her!!! They both like food and are talking about the food they like. Mr. Dan said he would cook her his favorite food from Libya. He brought it to school that day for her lunch. She said it was délicieux because of course she is learning some words in French now. I didn't think to put food in the PLAN! I think Ikran was knowing what Ms. Taylor said. Anyway she was happy too! And I told Jenna even though she doesn't work too much on the PLAN anymore.

Then I am thinking I can cook something from you

for Mr. Dan and Ms. Taylor for lunch someday. Will you tell me something I can cook for them? Or I will ask Mama too. This is a really good idea I think.

Bisous,

Anaïs

March 10

Dear Oma,

Miss said today in school that we will have Mud Season now. What is that you say? I also said What is that? Miss say Mud Season is when the snow melts and makes a lot of water in the ground and we get mud. Well, for sure, it is not like the rainy season at home. We have little rains here and not all together like in Congo. And it is true that the world is turning green very slowly. Mama, Jean-Claude and me saw a little bit of green by someone's door. Now we are looking for it all the time.

Now I will tell you one crazy thing about crazy Americans and rain. You will not believe it! In America rain makes people sad. They do not like the rain! Ikran and me are telling Ms. Taylor we love the rain in our countries. It makes us so happy to have water fall from the sky for drinking for us and our animals and for our gardens. Not like crazy sad Americans!

We talkd about rain because Ms. Taylor had a big bag of dirt on her table today. She said she was thinking it was time to plant seeds. Like you do in your garden! She say yes we will plant seeds like your Oma. We are going to keep them inside until it gets a little warmer. We planted yellow flower seeds and tomato seeds. The seeds were so tiny! We were very careful to put a little and not a lot of water on them.

Ms. Taylor was talking about the beautiful brown dirt. And Hassan say Red, Yellow, Blue! Ms. Taylor said yes. Bingo! I was thinking we are hearing this before all ready but then she was saying that letters can be blends too. Letters? Really? She was telling us that two letters can sound like themselves but also go together like CL in CLass, or FR in FRiend or SN in SNow to make one sound. We are thinking of blend words to write on our whiteboards when Ikran pointed to me and her. Friends she say. Ms. Taylor got a big smile. A blend is like two letters being two good friends. Another Bingo! Ikran looked very happy. That's nice

I'm thinking but I don't want to be a letter stuck to an Ikran letter forever!

I am thinking more about blends. Two things making one thing. So Ms. Taylor, I say. A person can maybe be a blend of two things? Like Africa and America in me? And Ms. Taylor said Yes and Bingo again and Very Very Cool! But I didn't say I was thinking how much of me is the Africa piece and how much is the America piece. I think maybe the American piece is only one very little toe.

Bisous,

Anaïs

March 13

Dear Oma,

We are sitting in our room at the shelter tonight drinking our sad tea. The tea is hot but my inside is cold and not good. We do not hear from Papa or Olivier. We do not know where they are. Mama tells me Papa and Olivier know what to do. They will run and hide and be safe. But Papa has a bad leg. And Olivier has a bad arm. And are there enuf places for them to hide in?

I hope you are safe and warm. I hope the stars are so so many and are smiling down at you. Please tell Monsieur to take care of you.

Bisous,

Anaïs

March 15

Dear Oma,

Guess what. Ikran is moving! Her family is finding an apartment in another part of the city so she will go to a new school. In my class with Ms. Taylor Hassan and I will be the only ones now. Ikran is annoying and like a little mama sometimes but I am seeing her here for a long time now. We are together a lot. It is going to be different when she is not here.

Miss said we will make cards for Ikran tomorrow. Ms. Taylor said we will also make cards in her class. And maybe we will have a party. Ikran knows the word for party. She looked happy about that. And Ikran asked Ms. Taylor if Mr. Dan can come. Yay for Ikran!

I am wondering what it will be like if Mama finds

a new apartment. She goes to look at apartments but doesn't find one yet. Many are too much money. I am happy to be at my school. I hope Mama can find an apartment near my school. I try to remember any place I go I will be like a blend of two letters or a blend of two countries. It helps sometimes. A little.

We said a prayer for Papa and Olivier in church yesterday. And I said one for you and Monsieur.

Bisous,

Anaïs

March 19

Dear Oma,

We had a party for Ikran today. Mama was helping me to cook manioc to take. Americans call it cassava leaves here. We put some white beans in too like you and Mama do. Ikran liked it and so did Ms. Taylor and Mr. Dan! Hassan not too much. Mr. Dan came with a bag of chips. He said he didn't have time to do some cooking. Ms. Taylor was bringing cheese and carrots and for dessert ice cream! Ikran loves loves loves ice cream so we have chocolate and strawberry ice cream! Ha ha, a blend of ice creams! Oma, I have to tell you that America can sometimes be crazy but one thing that is made really really good here is ICE CREAM! It is the one excellent thing about America today. It was a fun party. Mr. Dan

gave Ikran a card and Hassan and I gave her cards too. I hope she can read them. Hassan still writes kind of like spaghetti even when it is English and not Arabic. Ms. Taylor gave Ikran a card and also some very nice colored pencils and paper. I am thinking to myself this is what will happen if I go to another school too? Ikran was telling us about her new apartment and her new school. I'm thinking that is what she told us anyway. She talked but of course a lot was Somali. I have to tell you that I am sad she is leaving. She always came with me at recess and now I will need to play with other girls. Jenna and Brittany play together a lot. Maybe I can play with them.

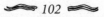

Do you hear anything of Papa or Olivier? I think about them all the time. Ms. Defazio helps Mama with the a silum papers. She says she wants to see the papers Papa has or talk to him. She hopes he can tell her more about why we can't go back to our country. She says she will maybe call you and Monsieur sometime too. I wish Papa was here right now so he can talk to her.

Bisous,

Anaïs

March 23

Dear Oma,

Spring is coming very very SLOWLY. Winter doesn't want to leave and spring doesn't want to come. At recess we can play outside on the tar but not on the playground yet because it is too wet there. Mud season I guess. I love to play jump rope. I am learning new ways to play it.

Today at recess I saw Mr. Dan and Ms. Taylor talking together in the parking lot. I wish I had Ikran to tell. I didn't hear any words they were saying but they were smiling. They look so so nice together! Then

Mr. Dan got in his car and Ms. Taylor went inside. I was telling Jenna the PLAN is looking good!

Next week is the school vacation. I will stay home for a week. Mama say we will go to the library and maybe go look at an apartment. If I go with her I can tell her if I like it or no. And maybe she will take us to Goodwill. She say maybe one night we will get a pizza for dinner too from the pizza place on the corner. Jean-Claude and I love pizza! It is round and is like a bread and it is red and white. It makes Jean-Claude a mess but it is so so good. When you come to America we will get you a pizza!

PIZZA!
(IT'S LIKE A BREAD &
IT'S RED & WHITE)

Do you hear anything from Papa or Olivier? We have not. Mama talks to her friends and calls on the phone but no one ansers. Sometime at night Jean-Claude asks me to tell him about Papa. I try to see Papa's face. I tell Jean-Claude Papa was away a lot of the time at his job but when he was home and when he smiled Papa had a big wide smile that made everything good and safe like sunshine. Then I don't tell Jean-Claude but I am seeing Mr. Dan's face instead. Is this bad? Am I forgetting? I go get Mama's phone and Jean-Claude and me hold it with the black rock inside it from Papa's mine and we look at Papa's smiling face in the picture.

Bisous and XOXO,

Anaïs

March 27

Dear Oma,

The Omar family is moving and I am very sad about it. They find a new apartment and suddenly they are putting things in boxes. We are helping because it is vacation week. I will miss Noor and Riham so much. They are my good friends here at the shelter and we ride the bus every day to school. I think it is like if I had little sisters. They are moving to another town not very near to here. We will have a party before they go and then I hope I will see them again sometime.

Mama has a hard time looking for an apartment for us. I think there are not too many apartments big for us in a place near here. Mama wants a place for Papa and Olivier to come to. And Mama say it has to be not too much money. So she looks and looks. I think she hopes if she finds an apartment then Papa and Olivier will come somehow.

Bisous,

Anaïs

April 1

Dear Oma,

Have you ever in your whole life been hearing of April Fools Day? Well I will tell you that it is today. April 1. It is of course one more crazy thing about America but funny too! When we go to school today Miss says the white tiles on the floor were cleaned with something speshal and we can only walk on the gray tiles all day. Did Mr. Dan do this I was thinking? So all the students are hopping and jumping from gray tile to gray tile for a lot of time trying to put our backpacks away and get our morning work. Brittany and me are bumping into each other and everyone is laffing.

Then Miss reads the morning message and it says April Fools Day!!!! I still do not know anything. Hassan too. But Januel says that it is a crazy thing they do in America to do jokes on April 1. Januel loves April Fools. So then we can walk on the white tiles again. It was really funny. The good funny!

When Hassan and me went to Ms. Taylor's class she said there was a spider under a paper cup on her table. She wanted us to help her get it outside! You remember I HATE spiders! They are so SCARY! And Hassan did not look happy too. But then I see she is smiling a little smile so I guess it was April Fools again! I was still afraid to look under the cup. Ms. Taylor put it in the trash. I was so happy to see no spider. I think Ikran will be laffing at this if she was here. I am guessing she has April Fools at her new school and I'm thinking she will not understand it at all! But she will have a lot to say in

Somali! I miss hearing all her Somali. I hope there is not
another April Fools until next year. Or some other crazy
American holiday!

Bisous,

Anaïs

April 4

Dear Oma,

Weekends are so boring! And now Noor and Riham are
not here to play with. I think a new family is moving in
to the empty room tomorrow. It is only us and the Potter
family. The one good thing is that Mama was giving me
new braids. Now I have many many beautiful braids and
colored beads on every one. I can shake my head and
hear them. I love the way they feel when I do this!

We do not hear anything from Papa and Olivier. Do
you? We think about what it will be like if we are all here
together. We went with Mama today to see an apartment
and I had to take care of Jean-Claude while Mama
talked to the woman. I told him a story about if Papa
and Olivier come. That room will be Papa and Mama's
room where Jean-Claude can sleep too. This one will

be Olivier's and this one will be my room. It was a nice story. I wish it will be true someday.

The apartment didn't look like it can be a house with stars I think. The woman say if we live here I will have to go to a new school. There is a school close to the apartment. She say it is a very good school but I know she is saying that because she wants us to like the apartment. I hate hearing about a new school. I know we need to move but I don't want to think about it. It makes me feel hot and cold like I eat something bad inside.

Then we go to the big food store. We are tired but we need to get the food. Has Mama told you about the big big food stores here in America? They are so big they are crazy! They are also one good thing about America for today. We put Jean-Claude in a shopping cart that looks like a car so you know he is happy. Then we walk this way and that way. There are walls of bags and boxes of food so high you cannot touch the top. There are mountains of oranges and apples and bananas. There is music coming from the roof. Jean-Claude and I ask Mama to get us a pizza and she said yes! The pizzas are in the cold, colder, coldest part of the store. The store people who work there put on there winter coats. It is like the Arctic or maybe the Antarctic. The penguins would be happy there. We

got a good pizza and got all the rest of our food in bags.
Mama had just enough money for us to take a taxi home.
We are so tired but we had a good dinner and watched a
movie from the library.

Bisous,

Anaïs

April 8

Dear Oma,

Guess what day it is today? Ha ha. It is my birthday!
I am 10 years old! It was so so good to talk to you
yesterday on the phone. You sound like you are right
here in America with us. I wish it was true!

I was happy to hear about what you are doing and
that you are happy at Monsieur's house and that you are
making his garden better than ever. When I see you in
my dreams you are working in Monsieur's garden or
maybe I can call it your garden now. I wish you are here
but I know you will not be happy if you have to leave
your garden.

Please call again soon if you can. I am so happy
to hear you talk and laff. And tell Monsieur we are

thanking him very much for trying to find out about Papa and Olivier. Mama does not hear anything.

I was hoping to get a card from Papa and Olivier. I know it is hard for them to do things like that and maybe they don't even remember it is my 10 year old birthday. Mama says they are thinking of me. She knows it. She says they will call as soon as they can.

At school today the students in my class are singing Happy Birthday to me. They clapd ten times for me and one more time so I have one to grow on. But I don't understand the grow on part.

Ms. Taylor and Hassan and I read a funny book about a birthday party. And she was bringing some brownies she had made. Brownies are chocolate and so so good. Mr. Dan came with a card and was eating a brownie too. He said it was the best one ever! I am happy Ms. Taylor and Mr. Dan are friends. It makes my birthday very happy. Ms. Taylor gave me brownies to take home too so we can have more birthday party at my home.

After school Mama was taking me and Jean-Claude to Goodwill to go shopping for my birthday. I got two tshirts, a new pair of blue jeans and a skirt with flowers on it. I am going to wear it tomorrow even if it is cold. Don't worry Oma. If it's cold I'll wear pants and my new skirt too. Jean-Claude wanted presents even though it is not his birthday.

I will look for some stars tonight. I will say Stars! I am 10 years old tonight! And I wish you will look down on Oma and Monsieur and Papa and Olivier wherever they are. I hope Papa and Olivier are knowing I am 10 years old today.

Bisous,

Anaïs

April 11

Dear Oma,

The new family is at the shelter now. They are from America. There is a mama, a little girl called Karla and a baby boy. I played with the baby today a little bit and Karla showed me one of her books. She wanted me to read it to her. It was a book for little kids but I still didn't know all the words. I made up some of the story.

One thing to tell you about was today when I was outside at recess. One of the teachers keeps a bird feeder outside and I lookd and was seeing a little yellow and black bird on it. Really you say? I look and look and it was true. The bird was smaller than our yellow and black birds at home but the same colors! I was telling Ms. Taylor and she said they are called goldfinches. She said they are a dark color in the winter but in summer or spring they turn brite yellow. She say I will see many more of them because they like to live here. I love goldfinches!

Bisous,

Anaïs

April 15

Dear Oma,

The best thing happened today! Jenna and Brittany asked if I can help them with a story. It is a new PLAN of Jenna. They see I like to draw and write. And they like my kursive writing because I do it so good! Because Monsieur was teaching me! They say it looks like the way princesses write. They are writing a story called PRINCESS SLEEPOVER! What is that I said? It is a story they said about princesses who have a very very fun sleepover. Real American girls love sleepovers when friends go to another friends house to sleep and play all night! And American girls really love princesses.

Jenna made a little book with many papers together. It is so fun! We write what the princesses will eat. Popcorn and hot chocolate and pizza. We write what the princesses will do. Watch tv, listen to music and put on fancy dresses. And fancy fingernails.

We write and color in our Princess Sleepover book before school and at free time. I am learning a lot about Princesses because I did not know about them.

We put 3 princesses in the story. Guess their names. Surprise! Brittany, Jenna and Annie Princess! Then I was starting to think about a problem. Princesses I think have long blond hair like Brittany. Maybe Jenna was thinking too. But then Brittany said the Brittany princess can have blond hair, the Jenna princess can have brown hair and the Annie Princess can have black hair with beads. Yay! I love Princesses!

Bisous,

Anaïs

The princess sleepover

April 19

Dear Oma,

Mama is talking to the people about the new apartment. She thinks it will be good to take it. It is big enough for when Papa and Olivier come. She say it is near a good school. She is filling out papers and seeing if there is money for it.

She tells me all the good things about it to try and make me happy. Like there will be more room for all of us. And Papa and Olivier will be here. Really? I want to ask when will they be here but I do not. I know she does not know.

And I can have my own room with a door. Sometimes I want it and sometimes I don't. So I don't think about it. I think about Princess Sleepover instead.

I will be sad to say goodbye to the new family with little Karla and the baby and even a little sad to say goodbye to the Potters and Hassan and his family on the floor below us. I am so tired of new new new. Most of all a new school. I am thinking princesses don't have to go to new schools or move to new apartments.

I had a dream of you last night sitting under your tree. I know every bit of it so well. And I see many many stars smiling in the sky. I wish we will have a house with stars too. I think, can you dream of me? Because you don't have a picture of where we are. I wish you can be here. If you were here it will be feeling more like home.

Bisous,

Anaïs

April 22

Dear Oma,

Oma, I almost can't believe it! I know you talked to Mama today when I am at school. Do you believe it? I wish I could hug you and dance with you because I am so happy. And I know you are too. So you know Papa called us today and Mama talked to him. Even Jean-Claude said hello to Papa and Olivier too. They are in Kenya Mama told me when I got home from school. They are in a refugee camp. I remember Ikran lived in a refugee camp in Kenya. It is so so big Mama says but at least they are safe and we can talk to them. And I can write letters and not worry about what I write!

I will tell everyone in school tomorrow. Ms. Taylor will be very happy too and maybe we can look on the computer for where Papa and Olivier are in Kenya.

I ask Mama when they can come to America. She looks a little sad. She says it will maybe be a long time. But Papa will try try try to get here. He said to Mama at least Olivier can go to school in Kenya so they are happy about that. And Papa say the doctors can look at Olivier's arm which still needs to get better. He said it is not doing too good but he will take Olivier to the doctors tomorrow.

Mama said that Papa and Olivier had one more very important very speshal thing to say. To me. It was HAPPY BIRTHDAY!

Bisous and XOXOXOXOXO

Anaïs

April 25

Dear Oma and Monsieur,
We talked to Olivier and it was so good to hear him on the phone! We tell him we miss him so much. I need to have a big brother again to tell Jean-Claude what to do because he does not listen to me! He told us it took a long long time to see a doctor but he and Papa did today. The doctors say they can fix Olivier's arm but they

have to operate and bandage it again. It will take some time but they say it will be good.

Today at school I tell Ms. Taylor about Olivier. Of course she has been hearing my stories about him before.

Mama is busy about the new apartment. She is busy with papers. I help with the cooking and with Jean-Claude and the cleaning but it feels like not very much.

Bisous,

Anaïs

April 27

Dear Oma,

We are not going to move to the new apartment. Mama talked to people at the apartment and the shelter. They said we do not need a big apartment if Papa and Olivier can not come yet. The big apartment is a lot of money too. Mama was very sad and was trying to let me not see the tears in her eyes. I think she was hoping if we got the apartment then Papa and Olivier will come. So here we are tonight thinking of you and Monsieur and Papa and Olivier and drinking our sad tea.

We talked about your house and tree and my house

with my tree house and the little yellow and black birds.
Are the people in our house liking my tree house? And
we remembered your garden. I hope you like the new
garden at Monsieur's house. We are all in new places.
Do you miss your home like I do? It is hard for both of
us I think. But I am glad you are with Monsieur. And it
is nice sitting here with Mama talking with our hot tea
even though it is sad too. I turned on the colored lights
tonight and I am pretending they are like real stars. I
hope there are stars smiling on you too.

Bisous,

Anaïs

April 29

Dear Oma,

The one good thing today is Princess Sleepover!
Jenna and Brittany and me have made pictures of the
princess dresses and what there homes look like. Each
one has a home called a palace. And guess what? My
palace for Princess Annie is a tree house! Jenna and
Brittany said it was so so COOL! It is the big bigger
biggest tree house ever with little yellow and black

birds all around it. And lots of little colored lights for if it is a cloudy night. I love it a lot and maybe someday I will live in a house like that!

I told Ms. Taylor about my palace and she was thinking we can read some other stories about princesses and write about them. She had one book with a white castle in it and pink clouds. It was the most beutiful ever but Hassan didn't think it was. So maybe we will read something else. But not soccer books!

Mama says to write hello. Hello. We got a letter from Papa and a letter from Olivier today! We are so happy to hear from them. I am trying to get Jean-Claude to write his name in a letter to them but it is hard for him.

Bisous,

Anaïs

May 2

Dear Oma,

Well Ms. Taylor says we will not write about princesses or about soccer because she say it must be something for both Hassan and me. She says she has a good idea. She says we can work on writing about our

Hopes and Dreams. What is our hopes and dreams I say? And she says it is like what we want to do when we are big and old. So I am thinking. You remember we talk like this under your tree before I am leaving? Maybe I want to be a doctor and help people. Like Olivier! But maybe I want to be a teacher. Ha ha, Monsieur will like this!

Hassan say he wants to be a soccer player and a pilot. Ms. Taylor asked him to pick one hope and dream. So he picked pilot. He is drawing a portret picture of him wearing a very fancy uniform. He really wants a gold crayon but we don't have one. The picture will have to be Hassan Pilot in just blue.

I tell Hassan I want to be a pilot too, ha ha. He gets mad and say only he can be a pilot and I'm a girl anyway. Ms. Taylor says I can be anything I want. She and I talk about I can be a artist or a teacher or anything. I don't know what to do! So for now I pick doctor because I think of Olivier and many people who are sick and need medicine.

I get to draw Annie Doctor but it is hard to draw a big white coat on white paper. It looks like my brown head legs and arms are sticking out of white paper! But I was drawing a very beautiful STETHOSCOPE. I learned

the word from Ms. Taylor. It's the thing doctors use to
listen to your breathing inside you.

Bisous,

Anaïs

May 5

Dear Oma,

Well you will never guess what a happy time has
come! Jenna and Brittany want to have a real Princess
Sleepover at Jenna's house! This will be the most funnest
thing ever!!! We will eat popcorn and pizza and soda
and wear some princess clothes I hope if Jenna can
find some. And we will watch tv and listen to music all
night. And go to sleep. Jenna said her mama will call my
mama. I write the number on a paper. I have to explain
princess sleepover to Mama. Mama is not sure if it's ok
but she says she will talk to Jenna's mama.

Ok I am writing about being a good doctor with Ms.
Taylor. Maybe I will send it to you when I am finished.
We are writing in paragraphs and drawing pictures. It
is called an SA but I don't know what that is. But Ms.
Taylor is helping Hassan and me. We are making a list
of why we want to be this. I want to help people. Hassan

say he wants to wear a nice uniform and fly a plane with a big engine because it will be cool. And fast.

   We all send big hellos to you and Monsieur. Now Jean-Claude is saying to me we have to write to Olivier to please come and play with him!

Bisous,

Anaïs

May 8

Dear Oma,

So it is night time and it is the night for the Princess Sleepover but you will not guess but I am not at Jenna's house. No I am in our room at the shelter. Jenna said her mama will call my mama but no call was coming. The phone didn't ring. Mama was thinking maybe her phone was not working or maybe the number was wrong. It was getting dark and still no ring. So now I am here with Jean-Claude and he is no Princess! It was going to be so so fun. Mama was trying to call Papa and then you too and the phone call was not working so she went to borrow a phone from a friend down the street and asked me to watch Jean-Claude.

Jean-Claude wants to play the Lost and Found game and I do not. I want to have a Princess Sleepover. I want Jenna and Brittany and popcorn and music. Hassan came and played with Jean-Claude so at least Jean-Claude is happy. They are doing something with little cars on the rug.

But I have nothing to do. So then I think I will have a Princess Annie Sleepover all by myself because if I don't I will be sad sad sad all night. And I am crying a little while all ready. No matter. We don't have popcorn but I can make hot chocolate and turn on the colored lights and watch a movie. And I draw a tree house palace with pink clouds. I put my soft animals and blanket on the floor like Pajama Day at school. Soon Hassan and Jean-Claude come see the movie too. So I am making more hot chocolate for us. The movie is about dinosaurs not princesses but it is a little funny. I'll be right back. Jean-Claude wants the hot chocolate.

Oma, here is sad news to tell you. I am writing from the hospital on a paper a lady gave me. You will never think what happened. We were watching the movie and Jean-Claude wanted hot chocolate so I went to cook the water. I went back to see the movie to wait for the water to get hot but then Jean-Claude went to the kitchen by his self. The water was really really hot. He was trying to pour it by his self before I got there and the big pot dropped and the hot water went all over him. He screamed and screamed. Hassan and I went and saw it. It was scary and very bad. Hassan was trying to help Jean-Claude but I told him to go get his parents fast and tell them to call 911. I took some of Jean-Claude's clothes off because they were hot too.

Hassan came back with his family. The Potters weren't home but the new family came. No one had seen Mama. They tried to call her but her phone is not working. Then the ambulance came. Everyone was yelling yelling. I told them the building of Mama's friend. Hassan looked at me and said he will find her. He ran out the door. The ambulance people were talking talking talking so many words and Jean-Claude was so hurt and scared and crying. They wanted to take him to the hospital but still Mama didn't come. They said they had to go. They started to take Jean-Claude but he was holding on to me. They said let go. I said no. I'm his sister. I have to go too. And I was holding on to the ambulance lady and Jean-Claude until she let me go too.

We went in the ambulance very fast. The loud siren noise scared Jean-Claude but I held on tite to him. I told the ambulance people what happened. I tell them his name and my name. One was using his phone. I ask for it and let Jean-Claude hold it. I tell him again how there is a little bit of black rock inside it from Papa's mine. Like a little bit of Papa himself.

In the hospital they let me go with Jean-Claude but then they said I have to let go. They said so many words. I didn't know what they are saying. They showed me a little room where I have to wait. And still Mama did not come.

So I sit by myself in this little room with very white lights and cold chairs. There is an old man and woman sitting there too. They are looking at me. I hear the man say to the woman Where are they all coming from? Why can't they stay in Africa? Is he thinking I do not have ears to hear him? Is he thinking I cannot speak English? Do I look stupid to them? They look at newspapers. So I take a newspaper too to show them I can read. But my eyes have much crying in them.

They leave and I sit there by myself. And no Mama. I was thinking did Hassan find her? Where is she? Will she come soon? Is Jean-Claude ok? What are they doing to him? I feel so so bad because I was watching the movie and not taking care of him. And I do not understand all the words the hospital people say. First

Papa got hurt then Olivier and now Jean-Claude. I cry cry cry and wish you are here. I wish Mama is here. I wish I was a doctor. I wish I was big and not only 10.

I think maybe the hospital people forget about me and I want to know how is Jean-Claude so I go into the hall to a desk. The desk is very tall and I can't see the woman behind the desk so I walk around it. Where is my brother? I say. She say What? I tell her his name but still she say What? I say Jean-Claude's name loud but all she say is What you say? Well I am sorry to say but then I am so so mad I have to yell Jean-Claude's name LOUD, LOUDER, LOUDEST!

I feel hands on me and I think they are taking me somewhere away and I want to see Jean-Claude more than anything. I don't want hands on me. I want Mama but she is not here so I need to look after Jean-Claude. I am trying so hard to get away but the hands hold me tite and a lady talks to me. She says a few words slow and I can understand them. It's ok she says it's ok. We'll find your brother. She says it over and over in a soft voice. I am still mad. She gives me tissues and a drink of water. She asks his name again and I help her write it on a piece of paper. Then she says the name to the desk woman.

She gets down to look at me and keeps her hand on me. She asks my name. I tell her my name and Jean-

Claude and Mama's name. She listens to everything I say.
I tell her I was looking at the movie and not Jean-Claude
and he hurt himself with the hot water. I tell her about our
home in Congo and that Olivier is with Papa in Kenya and
has a hurt arm and you sold your home so we can come to
America. She says something else to the desk woman and
soon a person comes who speaks French. And then Mama
comes with Hassan and his whole family! Hassan had run
and finally was finding Mama but they went to the wrong
hospital first. She was so glad to see me!

We went to see Jean-Claude who had many
bandages around his stomak. The doctors gave him
medicine and said he will be ok but they want to keep
him in the hospital for the night.

The nice lady is Mrs. Gonzalez. She and the man
who was speaking French stayed with us for a while.
She said to Mama she had never seen a girl who
was more DETERMINED than me. She was writing
DETERMINED on a piece of paper and gave it to me.

She said the way I stood in the hall with my hands
on my hips and yelled made her look up and listen right
away! You have a brave girl she told Mama. I whispered
to Mama I was sorry I was not watching Jean-Claude all
the time but Mama gave me a big hug anyway.

So we stayed with Jean-Claude in his room. Mama and I slept on a chair that turned into a bed. I will write more tomorrow.

Bisous,

Anaïs

May 9

Dear Oma,

We are still in the hospital waiting for the doctor to say Jean-Claude can go. When I get home I will send you my letters all together about Jean-Claude. Also with some pictures. I am drawing with Jean-Claude to make him happy. We are making a map picture of the apartment we will have some day. Jean-Claude wants dinosaurs in his room so I draw dinosaurs. Then he wants a soccer field outside so I draw that. And I draw stars because I want a house with stars. Real stars. Then he wants a table with a pizza on it so I draw that. Then Mrs. Gonzalez comes so I can stop drawing more pizzas! She stays with Jean-Claude while Mama and me go talk to the doctors and nurses. They talk to me and I help Mama understand the English. They show us what to do for Jean-Claude's bandages. Then we can go home.

Mrs. Gonzalez gives Mama her phone number. She tells Mama and me she is a lady at the hospital who helps people like us! She knows people at the shelter help us but she will also like to help us. She asks if she can come visit us soon to see how Jean-Claude is doing. I say yes even before Mama!

When we get home we use the phone of Mama's friend to call Papa and Olivier to tell them about Jean-Claude. Papa has many questions. I can hear he is so sad to be far far away from us. He wants to do something but he cannot. Olivier talks to Jean-Claude on the phone. That is nice for Jean-Claude. I can see he likes talking to his big brother.

Bisous,

Anaïs

May 10

Dear Oma,

I went back to school today. Jean-Claude is at home with Mama and he is feeling better. He wants to run and play but Mama tells him he cannot. He is not happy so

Mama lets him watch many movies. Last night Hassan was coming to play with him with the little cars and bringing Jean-Claude some little dinosaurs.

In my class we talk about what we did for the weekend. My class and Miss were very sorry to hear about Jean-Claude and the hospital! Hassan talked about it too. Jenna and Brittany said the Princess Sleepover wasn't lots of fun because Annie Princess was not there so they said we will have another princess sleepover soon. Yay!

Hassan and me went to Ms. Taylor's room and we told her about Jean-Claude too. We talked about it for some time and then worked on our hopes and dreams SA. I know now that we are writing ESSAYS about our Hopes and Dreams not SAs. But don't ask me what an essay is. I still don't know. Maybe Monsieur knows.

So I am thinking if I am a doctor when I'm older and bigger I can make children like Jean-Claude feel better when they burn themselves. I can fix bad arms for people like Olivier and know what medicine to give him. Maybe I can even fix Papa's bad leg. I am thinking a doctor will be an awesome thing to be! Maybe even better than a princess!

Ms. Taylor says she is glad I am good at math

because doctors need to work with numbers. I will
go finish my math homework now.

Bisous,

Anaïs

May 13

Dear Oma,

I was so happy today because Mrs. Gonzalez came to see
us. You will like her if you can see her. She is old but not
very old. And she is very nice. She smiles a lot and talks
so I can understand and she listens. She told us she came
to this country when she was a girl and she didn't know
English too! I told her we speak Lingala, French and
English or maybe a little English. She said it was awesome
to speak 3 languages! And she gave us a pineapple that
was cut up into little pieces so we can eat it with our
fingers!

She was glad to see Jean-Claude looking good.
She told him to be careful because he has to keep the
bandages on for a while. She said Mama was doing
a good job with the bandages. Mama told her I was

writing at school about being a doctor some day. Mrs. Gonzalez said that was excellent!

Mrs. Gonzalez talked to Mama again about what a good job I did at the hospital. She said I tell the doctors what they wanted to know in English. She said I have very good English and I was a big help to them! She said to Mama again that I was standing there with my hands on my hips looking very determined. And I was loud. She did what I did to show us. She was funny and very nice. Mama hugged me again and said she was very prowd of me.

Mrs. Gonzalez asked Mama if she can help her finding a new apartment for us. She will talk to the shelter people and other people she knows. She was bringing us the drawing I did for Jean-Claude in the hospital of the apartment we wanted! She showed Mama the dinosaurs and pizza and soccer field. And she remembered I want a house with stars. She and Mama talked about everything. Mama told her about Papa and Olivier in Kenya now and that they will come here some day.

And she left us the big pineapple to eat too!

Bisous,

Anais

May 16

Dear Oma,

Ms. Taylor and Hassan and me were looking at our two countrys on the computer today. Iraq and Congo. Then of course America too because it is our new country. It is so fun! Then we can see the whole earth and even the stars out in space! And they are the real stars not the little colored lights in our room.

And Mr. Dan was coming in the hall so he came and see the stars too. I tell them that you tell me before I leave our home that the stars will be smiling down on you and me together. We will both see the stars even if we live far far away from each other. Mr. Dan said he liked that maybe his brothers and sisters in Libya were seeing the stars too. I tell them that Mrs. Gonzalez is helping us look for an apartment now and she knows I like stars.

Bisous,

Anaïs

May 18

Dear Oma,

We get a letter from Papa today. He tells us about where
he and Olivier are living. He says he is trying to start
a little garden but he wishes you are there to tell him
what to do! He says there are many many people in the
refugee camp. He has met many people from Congo.
He is thinking about talking to a newspaper about the
mining company but told Mama he wants to be sure it
will be safe for him and Olivier. He said he has some
papers and pictures he was hiding that he will try to
copy and send them to us. He thinks Ms. Defazio will be
very excited about them! And they will help us for sure
get a silum here.

Jean-Claude is much better and running around a
lot. He only feels bad when Mama tells him to pick up
his toys. Then he looks sick and Mama picks up his toys
for him.

In school Miss is telling us about things we have to
do before the end of the year. She says it is coming soon
and we have to hurry hurry hurry and get our work
done! There is so much to learn she says! She says she
wishes she could feed it to us like mac and cheese. This

is something Americans love to eat. When I was new at school I was thinking it looked like throw up. Really! But I am telling you now that it is really really good. It is awesome!

We are learning about the ocean with Miss. Januel, Jenna, Brittany, Hassan and me are in one group so it is really fun. We can pick any ocean and write about it and draw pictures. And at the end of the year we will take a trip to the ocean here! Jenna and Brittany say it is a cool beach where we go and we can get in the water and eat food. Januel says he will make the biggest sand castle of all. Hassan says no he will. Maybe Jenna Brittany and me can make a Princess sand palace!

Bisous,

Anaïs

May 21

Dear Oma,

Well you will not believe it. But today Mrs. Gonzalez came with the shelter people and they are telling Mama about an apartment. Mama is going to look at it tomorrow with Mrs. Gonzalez. I am glad

Mrs. Gonzalez is going. She will help Mama know if it is a good apartment or not. The apartment is in another part of the city so I will have to go to another school. I think about Noor and Riham and Ikran. I guess someday I will have to move too for goodness sake. But now I guess a new school will not be too scary. I think I can do a new school ok.

My group is learning about the Atlantic Ocean at school. We picked it because it touches Africa and America and the island where Januel's family used to live. Only Hassan is not happy because it does not go to Iraq but we can not do anything about that for goodness sake!

We hear more from Papa about Olivier. The doctors operated on his arm and now it is in a cast. Ms. Taylor tells me about a cast. It is a thing that is very hard so Olivier cannot bend his arm. It has to stay like this so the arm gets better. But Ms. Taylor says it sounds like the right thing to do and someday Olivier will have a good better best arm! Olivier sent us a photo of his arm. Mama was glad to see him smiling anyway.

Bisous,

Anaïs

May 23

Dear Oma,

Mama and Mrs. Gonzalez liked the apartment a lot.
They say it is good for us. Not too big and not too small.
And not too much money. Mama has to fill out papers
with Mrs. Gonzalez and the shelter people and then we
will know if we move.

We are learning about waves and wind over the
oceans. Ms. Taylor is helping Hassan and me with our
resurch on the computer. Hassan still needs a lot of help.
Ms. Taylor shows him what to write. Sometimes at night
I help him copy what he has been writing. Because Ms.
Taylor ask me to do it. Then he plays with Jean-Claude
so it is good because I can do my math homework or
write to you and I don't have to watch Jean-Claude.

Mr. Dan came today for a few minutes because
Ms. Taylor said he can tell us about winds and waves
because he went over the ocean in his little boat! He said
sometimes the waves were looking bigger than school
busses! I am so glad he is safe. I think Ms. Taylor was
looking like she was very glad he is safe too. Ha ha! I am
thinking they are getting to be good friends all ready. I
tell Jenna and Brittany how they are doing.

We have not been hearing from you and Monsieur.
We hope you are ok and everything is good and safe
where you are? Mama tells me the soldiers have not
come back to your house I mean Monsieur's house. Is
Monsieur's cousin in the government making sure you
are ok? We think about you all the time.

Bisous,

Anaïs

May 27

Dear Oma,

Mrs. Gonzalez and the shelter people came today to
talk with Mama while I am in school to tell her we
can have the apartment! We will move there in a few
days. Hassan's mama and the new mama in the other
room and Mrs. Potter are helping Mama with boxes all
ready. Mrs. Gonzalez helped Mama with more papers.
Mama was telling her about Papa and Olivier too. Mrs.
Gonzalez asked if an American doctor can talk to a
doctor in Kenya about Olivier. She said she will also talk
to Ms. Defazio. She told us that if we get a silum then we
can ask to bring Papa and Olivier here too!

We were all so happy that Mrs. Gonzalez took us out for pizza! She said we had to CELEBRATE. She wrote the word for me. I was drawing a picture for you of us at the restaurant. You can see how much Jean-Claude loves pizza!

Bisous and XOXOXO!

Anais

May 31

Dear Oma,

I can stay at my school because it is almost the end of the year. I am so happy about that! The shelter bus can pick me up at 7:58 at our new apartment and then go to the shelter to get Hassan. Then after the summer I will go to my new school. I remembered today with Ms. Taylor what I was feeling on my first day. The school was so big and there were so many faces and words words words everywhere. An OCEAN of words!

Ms. Taylor says it won't be like that this time because she says I have learned so much English. I don't think I'm learning so much English like she says. Maybe she is saying it to make me feel better. She says we will do lots of speshal things before summer. And she says she will talk to my new teacher at my new school. I wonder how Ikran and Noor and Riham are doing at there new schools. Ms. Taylor asks if we are having a housewarming party for the new apartment. I say what is that for goodness sake? And she says it is a party when people come to celebrate a new home. I tell her Mama does not know about things like that in America but I tell her we sometimes have parties like that in my country.

Mr. Dan is also very sad I am leaving. He says he will miss having me to speak French with. I tell him he can speak French with Ms. Taylor. Ha ha. And then for goodness sake he was telling me she is already helping him with his English homework from his night time school! That is making me very happy for today.

Bisous,

Anaïs

June 4

Dear Oma,

Well I want to write that we moved into the new apartment and here we are in it right now. But I am not sure yet if it is the one good thing for today. Everything here feels so so new and different. We have to learn about the heater and the lights and the keys and the scary washing clothes place in the basement. There is a lot to learn from our new landlord. Mrs. Gonzalez is helping us.

We have a table and chairs and a sofa and two beds. Mama and Jean-Claude sleep in one room and I sleep in another room. And we have our own kitchen. That is so so nice! The food in the refrigrater is ours from Mrs. Gonzalez and no one else will eat it. Like Mr. Potter! Mama can cook now all by herself. Maybe she will make us bread and manioc tonight. But maybe we will also have the pizza and ice cream Mrs. Gonzalez was bringing us!

It is much more quiet than the shelter. No Potter family or the new family with the little baby crying in the other room. We are all alone in the apartment. Even Jean-Claude is quiet tonite.

You remember you tell me we will find a home some day? And it will be different from our old home but I will know it is the rite home for us? You tell me a home is waiting for us? I am thinking about this apartment and looking at it. I do not know if it is the rite one. It does not feel like home yet.

I am going to put up the little colored lights. The apartment needs to have stars. We do too.

Bisous,

Anais

June 7

Dear Oma,

I am waiting to write that the apartment is the one good thing about America today. I have not desided yet. It does not feel like home yet. I don't know why. The colored lights help but it's not rite. Not yet.

At school we are getting ready for our trip to the beach. We made our report on the Atlantic Ocean yesterday to the class. Ms. Taylor came to see it. It was really good and the class liked it and clapped! I did my best cursive writing for copying the facts Jenna and Brittany were finding on the computer. Januel did the map. It was very cool exept that he made his island really big said Miss. And Hassan was drawing the animals and fish that live in the Atlantic. Of course he was drawing a Killer Whale too!

It was a good day.

Papa sent us a picture today from his phone of him

and Olivier together. They are both smiling and looking happy. Papa is holding up a little tiny green leaf from his garden and Olivier is holding up his arm in the cast. Mama says we will get a big big copy of the picture and put it up on our wall.

Bisous,

Anaïs

June 10

Dear Oma,

Our trip to the beach was today! The beach is one good thing about America for sure! You will ask about the new apartment I know. It still does not feel like home yet. But the beach was AWESOME! We picked up seaweed and little dead crabs and rocks. We know about these things from learning about the ocean. The seaweed was so disgusting! But I loved the sand. It was warm so we can take off our shoes. I wear shoes so much in America

SEAWEED
IS SO DISGUSTING

I forget how good it is to walk with nothing on my feet! The water was very very COLD. The new word for today is FREEZING. But it was still fun to run in and out of the water. And the waves were tiny. Not like the school bus waves Mr. Dan talked about! These waves were more like the little toy cars Jean-Claude and Hassan play with!

Jenna and Brittany and me made towers of sand with buckets. Januel and Hassan were trying to build the biggest sand castles of course. The sand castles were always falling down. Ha ha!

The last day of school is coming soon and we say goodbye to everyone. I am making a card tonight for Ms. Taylor and one for Miss and one for Mr. Dan.

Bisous,

Anais

THE *beach* IS GOOD THING FOR AMERICA FOR SURE! (THE BEACH WAS AWESOM!)

June 16

Dear Oma,

Well the last day of school is today and it was a sad day. It came and go go go so fast! First we give out all our cards to Miss and she say how AWESOME we all are. Miss gave us hugs and talked and talked. She still say so many many words so fast! And we are in grade 5 now! Then we clean out our desks and put everything into BIG bags. We find many things that we lost a long time ago. I find my good eraser! We clean our desks and chairs. Januel told us he is moving too. To another part of America so no more Poison Girls Club or sand castles for Januel. I will miss Januel. He was funny. We say goodbye to him. We say goodbye to everyone.

Ms. Taylor made brownies and we have them today at school. It was me and Ms. Taylor and Hassan and Mr. Dan. We are talking about coming to America and about my new school. Ms. Taylor is giving me her email address so I can write to her on the computers at the library then she can tell Mr. Dan how I am doing. I was telling them some of the crazy things about American schools when I was new. They laffed when I showed them I was thinking the school lunch looked like something from my nose! Ms. Taylor said some things are a little crazy for sure but she said I know so so much now that my new school will not be so crazy. I am hoping she is right.

I am telling them too about how you and Monsieur make me look for one good thing about America every day! I was thinking you were crazy and some days it was a very very hard job! They wanted to know what are some of the one good things and I tell them Ice Cream, Pizza, Goodwill, Sledding, the Library, and Ms. Taylor, and Mr. Dan too and I wasn't remembering all of it for sure.

And then, you will not guess what they said, but Ms. Taylor and Mr. Dan both said I WAS ONE GOOD THING ABOUT AMERICA FOR SURE! Me I said? Are you Crazy? No, said Ms. Taylor. She was smiling a very big smile. And she said you know all those good things will be at your new school too, right? I love Ms. Taylor and Mr. Dan. I wish you will meet them some day. Maybe some day when I am a doctor I can bring you and Monsieur to America. When I tell Ms. Taylor this Hassan says and he can fly you here because he will be a pilot. Ha ha!

I am in the apartment writing to you. Mama is

cleaning the apartment but I don't know why because she cleaned yesterday. I am trying to keep Jean-Claude busy. I miss school all ready and I only got back an hour ago.

Bisous,

Anaïs

June 17

Dear Oma,

Well you will not believe this for sure. Even I can't believe it and I am right here! After I was writing to you yesterday Mama finished her cleaning and started to get dinner ready. And then the new doorbell was ringing and it was Mrs. Gonzalez and Ms. Defazio. I was happy to see them because the last day of school was kind of sad. Also, they were bringing pizza. They said they are putting their heads together to get us a silum and then we can ask to get Papa and Olivier here too! Putting their heads together? Really?

But before I can ask them how they do that the doorbell rang another time and guess what? It was Hassan's family coming with Noor and Riham's family, the Omars! They came up all the stairs to the apartment and were bringing food. It was the biggest surprise but Mama had a big secret smile on her face. She said Ms. Taylor had called her and was telling her about a housewarming party and that she wanted to give us one in the new apartment! I can not believe it for sure! But then Ms. Taylor came with Mr. Dan for goodness sake and she said the same thing. So we had a housewarming party right here in the new apartment. Mr. Dan was bringing flowers and everyone was bringing food. Jean-Claude was so happy to see Hassan he gave him a big hug.

Ms. Taylor had called Ikran and her family came too! It was a big big surprise. It was so so fun seeing her again. Ikran says she likes her new school. She even knows a little more English now. Yay! And she said a lot more too about her new school I guess but I don't really know because of course it was in Somali.

And Ms. Taylor had even talked to Brittany and Jenna and they came with their families. I can not believe it! Jenna and Brittany and Ikran and I were so happy to see each other. Some of Mama's friends came from her English class, too. And some of our church friends. And the Potter family came too. Any place there is a lot of food is a good place for Mr. Potter. And of course he still says Whatszup any time he sees me! There was so many people in our little apartment but it was so fun. Everyone was talking in English, Arabic, French, Somali with a little Spanish from Ms. Taylor and a little Italian from Mr. Dan too. And eating! There was vegetables and cooscoos and spicy chicken and sambusas and manioc and Mama's bread and rice and chips and pizza and one big cake from Ms. Taylor with a picture of a house on it!

When it got late our friends had to go. Everyone was cleaning up and getting their plates. Brittany and Jenna's mamas talked to Mama and made sure they got her phone number so we can see each other this summer. Jenna says we still have to have a Princess Sleepover! I will miss Noor and Riham and Ikran. Jean-Claude will miss Hassan for sure but Mama says we will see them again. Hassan's mama said maybe we can all go see this beach Hassan keeps talking about. And Hassan remembered he still has my black backpack with the yellow and black bird on it. He said he will give it back so I can take it to my new school.

Mrs. Gonzalez was going but I know we will see her again. She was talking with Ms. Taylor and telling her that seeing me at the hospital made her want to help us. Ms. Taylor was smiling and saying yes yes that sounds like Anaïs!

While the other families cleaned up, I went down the stairs with Mrs. Gonzalez and Ms. Taylor and Mr. Dan to say goodbye at our door. We hugged and said good night and shook hands and hugged again. Mr. Dan said if we need something fixed in the new apartment we can call him anytime. Ms. Taylor said she'd be in touch and I'm not sure but I think that means I'll see her again soon.

And then Mrs. Gonzalez said Anaïs Look at the Stars! I looked and saw a hundred thousand million stars out tonight. Real stars! I hope you saw them too, Oma. Mrs. Gonzalez said you've got your house with stars Anaïs!

I didn't say that I still wasn't sure if it was really the right house for us. If it was really the home you said I will find some day. But I saw the stars in the sky and the colored lights in our apartment and all our friends in the windows and I am thinking the apartment feels better now.

So then Ms. Taylor blue me a kiss and she and Mr. Dan went one way because I think they came together.

Ha ha! And Mrs. Gonzalez waved and went the other way.

I was standing in the door Oma and thinking about tonite and all the people in our little apartment. I keep losing count because there were so many! I am so happy.

We have a big picture of Papa and Olivier on our wall now. When they come we will show them our friends, our apartment and all the one good things about America. And someday you and Monsieur will come and see it all, too.

Ok, Oma, I have something to tell you. I was seeing the colored lights in our open windows and hearing Mr. Potter laff and Jean-Claude cry for goodness sake. So I was remembering the Halloween house with stars and how it was filled with stars yes but people too. The stars were so pretty that I was forgetting about the people! Oma, I have to tell you there is something better even than a house with stars. It is a house filled with friends! And some stars too for sure. BINGO!

Bisous and XOXO

Anais

For more information on this story's topics, here are a few websites:

http://www.our-africa.org
SOS Children's Villages is a global children's charity that cares for orphaned
and abandoned children in 45 African countries. This website has information
and some films made by children about life in many African countries.

http://www.unhcr.org/en-us
UNHCR is the UN Refugee Agency. For 65 years it has helped more than
50 million refugees successfully restart their lives in 126 countries.

http://www.unicef.org
The United Nations Children's Emergency Fund provides aid to children
and mothers in developing countries. On this website there are stories about
children in many parts of the world.

https://www.uscis.gov
This is the website for the U.S. Citizenship and Immigration Services. There
is detailed information for those seeking asylum and for refugees on how to obtain
a green card and how to apply for naturalization, the term used for the
process by which U.S. citizenship is given to a foreign citizen.

A NOTE FROM THE AUTHOR

When I stepped into an English Language Learning (ELL) classroom in Auburn, Maine, during an author's visit several years ago, I encountered for the first time the wonderful eagerness, curiosity and humor of ELL students. It was the spark that pushed me to go back to graduate school for a master's degree in teaching with ELL certification.

One of my internships took me to the Intensive English Language Development class at King Middle School in Portland, Maine, where the goal was to help new students learn enough English to move into mainstream classrooms. During that year (2012–13) we had newcomers arriving almost every other week. There was an amazing mix of cultures, ages (grades 6–8), and languages. At any one time, students were helping one another in Somali, Arabic, French, Portuguese, and English. When a visitor came to the class, the students would introduce themselves, name their country of origin, and say how many languages they spoke. It was usually three and sometimes four or five!

Working with them, I got to see and hear firsthand their determination to learn English and to figure out how to be a teenager in this new American culture. I loved hearing their stories and helping them with their schoolwork. Their resilience was awe-inspiring.

Since 2013, I have worked in an elementary school in South Portland, Maine, in the ELL department. Some students are newcomers to this country, some have been in the United States for years, and some were born in the U.S. but speak another language at home. We have students from every continent except Australia and Antarctica!

Because it takes approximately five to seven years to become fluent in both basic and academic English, we often work with the same students over several years. It has been such an honor to watch them grow, to work and laugh with them, to hear about their cultures, to answer their many questions, and to meet their families.

In writing this story, I wanted to give readers a glimpse of what it is like for a brand-new student to arrive in an American school from another culture. I hope readers will see that newcomers who are trying to navigate life at school have often left family and friends at home in their native country. Some have gone through a lot of hardship to get here. They have so much to learn and to process while they are still children! I can only say that we are lucky to have them here. New students bring other parts of the world to our doorstep. The richness of their cultures that they bring helps all our students learn to respect differences and to appreciate how much we have in common. Students with different backgrounds work together in the classroom and play together at recess. They share stories and jokes. At the same time,

I hope readers will see American schools through a new lens. Some of our routine events (Pajama Day) and slang ("cutting" in line) can be pretty funny!

This story is fiction, and no one character is based on any one of my students. The characters are blends and mixtures of people I have met and worked with. Almost all of what happens at the school in my story has been directly inspired by what I've encountered in the schools where I've worked.

There is, of course, no way I can truly know the experiences of a refugee or an asylum-seeker. But I have tried to document what I have witnessed over the past five years and to bring alive the kind of story that so many students are living. And one day soon, my hope, and expectation, is that my students will write their own stories. I can't wait to read them.

ENGLISH WORDS ANAÏS IS LEARNING

what she hears	the spelling she will learn	what she hears	the spelling she will learn
all ready	already	cande kanz	candy canes
anser	answer	can no	cannot
April Fools Day	April Fools' Day	clapt	clapped
are	our	cloze	clothes
a silum	asylum	confernses	conferences
askt	asked	cooscoos	couscous
bananes	bananas	countrys	countries
batroom	bathroom	desided	decided
beutiful, butiful	beautiful	diffrent	different
bisicles	bicycles	dont	don't
bleu	blue	enuf	enough
blue	blew	everytime	every time
bole	bowl	exept	except
brand new	brand-new	fish bowl	fishbowl
brite	bright	fite	fight
busses	buses	for evere	forever
cafeterya	cafeteria	forth	fourth

what she hears	the spelling she will learn	what she hears	the spelling she will learn
frend	friend	tine	tiny
Froste Snowman	Frosty the Snowman	tite	tight
goodnight	good night	tonite	tonight
gos	goes	treeting	treating
Hanika	Hanukkah	trik	trick
happyer, happyest	happier, happiest	triying	trying
hear	here	ware	wear
hisself	himself	workd	worked
hole	whole	worryed, worryd	worried
kindrgarten	kindergarden	xtenshuns	extensions
kostooms	costumes		
kursiv, kursive	cursive		

FRENCH WORDS

French words	English translation
absolument	absolutely
au revoir	good-bye
bananes plantain	bananas that are good for cooking
bisous	kisses
Bonjour, Mademoiselle	Good morning, Miss
Bonne Année	Happy New Year
bonne nuit	good night
ça va?	How are you?
complètement fou	totally crazy
dégoutant	disgusting
délicieux	delicious
énervant	annoying
ennuyeux	boring
étoiles, les	stars
français, le	the French language
frites	French fries
hippopotames	hippopotamuses
Joyeux Noël	Merry Christmas
Père Noël	Santa Claus or Father Christmas
voyelles	vowels
vraiment	really

(continuation of left column "what she hears" / "the spelling she will learn")

what she hears	the spelling she will learn
Kwonza	Kwanzaa
laff, lafft, laffing	laugh, laughed, laughing
langage	language
learnd	learned
listend	listened
lookd	looked
mabe	maybe
mayke	make
oshun	ocean
pickd	picked
playd	played
potatos	potatoes
prowd	proud
refrigrater	refrigerater
rite	right
SA	essay
Santa Cloz, Santa Clouz	Santa Claus
showd	showed
sleding	sledding
smilie	smiley
speshul/speshal/speshel	special
stayd	stayed
stomak	stomach
stuffd	stuffed
there	their